For ann Mayer

On memory of my visit to
The national Medal of Honor
museum - Pigeon Forge

11-16-2000

Sincerely
Robert L. Burlingame

APPALACHIAN HAVEN

I write, publish (under my own THRIFTECON PUBLICATIONS), and distribute my own books. This book was first published in 1981 and has been very well received. But many persons who were part of this book in 1981 are now deceased, and some who are now a part of my life were not then born. Please refer to page viii on reverse of dedication page for details.

THE AUTHOR

APPALACHIAN HAVEN

BY ROBERT L. BREEDING
DOCTOR OF EDUCATION

THRIFTECON PUBLICATIONS

Col. Robert Breeding
405 Ascot Ct
Knoxville TN 37923-5807

(815) 539-9932

First printing 1981
Second printing 1992

FRONT COVER DESIGN BY MARVIN THOMPSON

Library of Congress Cataloging in Publication Data

Breeding, Robert L.
  Appalachian Haven
  Bibliography: p. 279
  1. Tennessee --History--Fiction.   I. Hurst, Shirley J.
II. Title
PS3552.R364J6   813'.54   81-2312
                            AACR2

ISBN 1-880258-00-5

APPALACHIAN HAVEN

Linking present to past and fact to fiction, the author, born and reared in a remote part of southern Appalachia, seeks answers to many questions: why do his personal genealogical studies dead-end in eighteenth-century Virginia; why and how did his ancestors and those of other southern highlanders originally settle in the mountains; and why have large numbers of their twentieth-century decendants clung to the pioneer lifestyle of over two hundred years ago?

The perspective gained in half a lifetime spent in far places authenticates this product of years of detailed research for logical answers to these questions. Three different parts comprise this book; a lavishily illustrated personal recollection of a mountain boyhood; the report of a recent return to the area to find it virtually unchanged after fifty years; and an imaginative story, solidly based upon historical fact, which logically explains why and how his eighteenth-century forebears chose to settle in his hidden valley.

Cherokees and Melungeons; learned Londoners, indentured servants, and white Indian captives; London slums, Tidewater Virginia plantations, and perilous pioneer trails—all these, together with extensive treatments of customs, religions, and differing philosophies, are found in this fascinating explanation of the origins of countless modern Americans who claim hillbilly antecedents.

☆ THE EDITOR ☆

For Joyce
&
Carolyn and Sharon
&
Robert Lynn and Robert Lynn, Jr.
&
Rose, Christian, Emma, and Maggie
&
Sam and Ken

NOTES TO THE READER

Since its first publication in 1981, some changes surrounding personnel involved with this book (at its second printing in January 1992), are as follows:

> My late son, Robert Lynn Breeding (listed on the Dedication Page) died of cancer on October 6, 1982

> Marvin Thompson, (who designed the cover for this book) died of a heart attack.

> Dr. James E. Arnold,(who wrote ABOUT THE AUTHOR, page 277) died of a heart attack.

> Dr. Harry M. Caudill, (whose endorsement appears on the back cover of this book) is deceased.

> Ms. Shirley M. Hurst, who edited this book, has had a heart valve replaced and is disabled.

>The author has had a 4-graft heart by-pass.

> Of my five grandaughters, two were born since this book was first published. They are (1) Emma Ruth Groce, born December 20, 1981, and (2) Maggie Baker, born July 19, 1983.

> I have adapted this book for young adults, ages 10 to 14, and published it under the title FROM LONDON TO APPALACHIA.

ACKNOWLEDGMENTS

The idea for this book germinated over a span of years and matured only when I devoted my full time and energies to research and writing. After long hours of searching and checking thousands of sources, I could name literally dozens of books that influenced what I have presented in this book. For the sake of brevity, however, I will name only a few of these: Harry M. Caudill's *Night Comes to the Cumberlands;* Abbott Emmerson Smith's *Colonists in Bondage;* and Herma Cate, Clyde Ussery, and Ramsey Armstrong's *The Southern Appalachian Heritage.*

Mr. Caudill and personnel at Little, Brown and Company have given me permission to quote some information from that source and I express to them my thanks and appreciation. I heartily recommend the reading of all of Mr. Caudill's books by persons interested in the general geographic habitat and plight of the southern highlander or "hillbilly."

x • ACKNOWLEDGMENTS

Although I have not quoted directly from Smith's *Colonists in Bondage*, I recommend it as one of the most authentic and outstanding books in its field. I have used it very liberally as a major source. The third book specifically mentioned, Cate-Ussery-Armstrong's *The Southern Appalachian Heritage,* is an absolute must for those who want to understand and enjoy *Appalachian Haven.* I did not discover that book until very late in my research, but when I bought a copy and read it I found it a most rewarding experience. I found that it not only gives an outsider a different view of the hillbilly heritage and way of life, but also it espouses much of the very same philosophy that I was trying to formulate and express. I have permission to quote from that source also.

An express and specific note of thanks is directed to Mr. John Van Mol, former Director of Information of the Tennessee Valley Authority, Knoxville, Tennessee, and his staff for providing many of the photographs that appear throughout this book; and to Mr. Lewis E. Wallace, Deputy General Counsel for TVA at Knoxville, for authorizing their use. Those photographs are identified in pages following. (It is my understanding that most of the TVA photographs were made by Lewis W. Hine about 1933). Also, I wish to thank relatives and friends who donated and authorized the use of family photographs; and of course I have some of my own family photographs as well.

I am extremely grateful to Dr. Duane H. King, Director of the Museum of the Cherokee Indians,

Cherokee, NC. for having read this manuscript and for having specifically commented on those portions dealing with the history, geography, customs, and lifestyle of the Cherokee Indian of the time period in which this book is set.

I have included a long bibliography of the various sources which were of special help in my research, but I must emphasize that such books as Kephart's *Our Southern Highlanders,* Brewer's *Valley So Wild,* Rothrock's *French Broad-Holston Country,* and the books of Dykeman, Marius, Raulston, Mason, Brooks, Campbell, Chase, Malone, Ogburn, Tunis, Buckley, and Barth were of extreme importance. The debt which I owe to those writers cannot be paid by mere words. Also, I direct your attention to the footnotes which specifically identify major sources of explanations. Some extracted materials have been placed in appendixes to provide details necessary for certain accountings. It is well to remember, however, that a writer cannot recall every single source used, but rather he (she) specifically credits major sources which verify a particular idea. For example, the information about early European civilization, the Roman church and the papacy, the Renaissance and the Reformation, and early American settlements is of such common knowledge that even the author cannot remember its source. I do, however, acknowledge that such material is in no way an invention of mine, and credit must be given to the historians who compiled it over the years.

Lastly, I acknowledge the tolerance, patience, and frank criticisms of my wife (and lover) for the past forty-nine years. Without that the laborious, but gratifying, task of writing this book would have been far less pleasant.

CONTENTS

* APPENDIXES SPECIFIED ON NEXT PAGE

APPENDIXES

ILLUSTRATIONS

*OFFICIAL IDENTIFICATION AND SOURCE OF EACH PHOTOGRAPH IS LiSTED WHERE KNOWN. PHOTOGRAPH CAPTIONS IN TEXT ARE THE AUTHOR'S COMMENTS, IN CONTEXT WITH THEIR USE.

M. TVA Photograph H-29. Pyles Homestead. Andersonville, Tn. 10/25/33.

N. TVA Photograph H-34. Harriett Hankins' home near site of Norris Dam. 10/25/33.

O. TVA Photograph KX-490-no Identification. 1933.

P. TVA Photograph H-67. Home of Alfred Bledsoe on Cedar Creek near Loyston, Tn. 10/31/33. Cabin was about 100 years old).

Q. TVA Photograph K-401. No Identification. 1933.

R. TVA Photograph KX-7568. No Identification. 1933.

S. Author's home—about 1935.

T. TVA Photograph KX-621. No Identification. 1933.

U. Ridge School near Lone Mountain, Tn. About 1934. Courtesy Irene Bundren.

V. TVA Photograph H-24. Oakdale School, Loyston,

W. Tn. 10/31/33.

X. Author's brother Clyde. 1938.

Y. Left: Author's mother and sister Dora-1938.

Y. Right: Author's mother and father - 1944.

Z. Family group - 1936.

ILLUSTRATIONS (cont'd)

PREFACE

The southern highlander, or "hillbilly," is characterized by peculiar (different) habits, language, customs, and lifestyle; by seemingly inbred overwhelming
desire to do things his way both when and where
he wants to; and by an innate intelligence that has
nurtured his culture for more than two hundred years.

The celebration and national attention given our
nation's two hundredth birthday, the public acclaim
of such novels as Alex Haley's *Roots,* and the publication of numerous research endeavors to discover
and publicize the origin of various regional and family
groups have all served largely to heighten and sharpen
my longtime interest in the origin and ancestry of the
southern highlander, or hillbilly. Paradoxically, I
had been engaged in research for this book more
than five years before our bicentennial celebration,
and my efforts not only served the purpose for which
I first undertook them but also culminated in bringing
some bits of my own family history into a sharper
focus.

I have thoroughly and meticulously researched
the material for this book, and the footnotes and
appendixes verify its historical accuracy and authenticity. I am not so naïve as to ask the reader to believe
every detail presented, since I have taken the liberty
of injecting names and characters into the scenario
(and even, in some cases, altered the scenario) to
suit my own fancy, but rather I ask him to accept
the authenticity of the framework of history as presented.

My research began with a general, stereotyped
survey of the habitat of the southern highlander,
and why and how his historical and geographical
place has influenced his peculiar lifestyle. I found
very quickly, however, that I needed to identify that
lifestyle and to show that it was not necessarily inferior to other specific lifestyles, but rather, in many
ways, only different. To accomplish that end I decided
that my best course lay in recording the reality of
what it was like to grow up in that culture fifty years
ago and in following with a description of a revisit
to that area in 1976, when I verified that many of
the inhabitants, and their living conditions, had changed very little over the intervening fifty years. After
writing those parts, mostly from personal knowledge
and experience, I became more and more curious
about the specific history of the ancestry of that group
of people prior to the 1930s. Therefore, I researched
and wrote the fictional but historically accurate version
of Jamie's story that is found in Part 3 of this book.

The table of contents outlines Jamie's story, which delineates the historical and economic reasons that propelled certain people from Europe to Appalachia. Also, this story not only recounts why and how the first white people came to southern Appalachia, but it also expands that account to the point of shedding a great deal of light on the history and habits of the Cherokee Indian, as well as other historical and geographical events of that time. Jamie's settlement in the southern highlands, his two marriages, and the rearing of several offspring is also believed to have some possible connection with my own family ancestry.

In retrospect, I became interested in why many of our earliest settlers came to the New World with the customs, habits, and ways of thinking that they did. Having researched the subject thoroughly, I had intended to present, as Part 4 of this book, my version of history's reason for the occurrence of these happenings as they came about. However, the complexity of the subject indicated that it deserved treatment in depth. Therefore, in the future I intend to expand what would have been a section into a full-length book because I feel that there are many people who, like myself before I completed this research, have not taken the time and trouble to read and analyze the history of the Middle Ages with the view of developing a cause-and-effect theory linking that historic period to the early history of the United States.

Photographs interspersed throughout this book

are not intended, for the most part, to describe, identify, or pinpoint specific people and places, nor are they intended in any way to be degrading and derogatory. Rather it is hoped that they will serve the intended purpose of depicting generalities of the southern highlands and its people at specified times in their seemingly happy existence, still largely tucked away from the hustle and bustle of the outside world.

Part I

In Early Years

A. SOME HISTORY AND GEOGRAPHY

In this aftermath of bicentennial thinking, when a great deal is being said about our nation's heritage, one is naturally caused to wonder about his own personal heritage, as well as the heritage of the group of which he is a part. The heritage of the southern highlander (commonly referred to as the hillbilly) is uniquely representative of some of the earliest American pioneer culture, and many millions of modern Americans can relate some of their background to that pioneer cultural heritage.

Geographers generally refer to the southern highlands as the mountainous portions of the upper and middle south, or mountains of Tennessee, the Virginias, Kentucky, Georgia, and the Carolinas. Such general references are made to the mountains and foothills of the southern Appalachian chain, and even the mountains of the Blue Ridge and the Cumberlands. This area is the natural habitat of the native southern highlander, generally referred to, over the years, as a hillbilly. In some cases, depending largely on the person making the reference, geographic areas so designated encompass the major portions of a state or group of states, and thus often are not easily differentiated from nearby metropolitan areas, most of which are not considered to be occupied by hillbillies. In fact, the old-timer hillbilly himself generally professes to believe that such urban areas are inhabited by foreigners or aliens.

It is a generally accepted thesis that most American frontier areas were settled, originally occupied by the white man, or wrested from the Indians by white people who moved westward to enjoy plentiful land and virgin territory and resources, while at the same time their alleged reasons for doing so were to seek their fortunes or escape some unwanted restriction of their current society. For example, it is generally held that the Puritans of New England braved the harshness of a new and unknown world in order to escape societal and church restrictions of Old World societies and cultures. They deliberately chose to live in a strange, new environment in order that they might live, speak, and do what they wanted and believed in. In that time, and in the years immediately thereafter, in most American frontier areas the pioneer sought land and space where he could sustain himself and his family, and live in a manner suited to his liking. As rapidly as the *old* places became settled, crowded, and unlike what the pioneer wanted and sought, just so rapidly did he set out westward to find *new* places more to his liking.

Usually, when he found these *new* places, that is, when he had created a new westward frontier, he first engaged in establishing rules and guidelines to govern his new society; then he began a systematic effort to create the safety of a stable society for himself, his family, and his neighbors. To the American pioneer family the frontier, for the most part, was simply a passing phase which preceded the establishment of so-called "civilization," with its inherent opportunities to live according to their own rules, enjoy a society of their own making, amass wealth or some sort of material possessions, and propagate their own particular religious beliefs. Generally speaking, those frontiersmen who could not adapt to such a civilization simply moved on to newer westward frontiers, thus contributing to the establishment of still newer societies.

In general, the same thesis holds true regarding the southern highlander, or hillbilly, except for three major differences. First, the frontiersmen who first occupied the southern highlands were rooted in a different cultural background; that difference comprises the main theme of this book. Secondly, they did not think of the frontier as a passing phase beyond which they must journey to a better time and place. Thirdly, they wanted no set rules and guidelines by which to be governed. On the contrary, their actions indicated a belief that they had found their *Promised Land*, and they cherished the freedom and savage harshness of that early primitive existence, seemingly using their mountains as treasured hideaways. Being passionate seekers and lovers of freedom, they seemed resolved to avoid the mildest limitation which any kind of organized society would impose on their liberty. Any slightest manifestation of government apparently was abhorrent to them, since it reminded them of the unwanted restrictions from which they had just fled. Far from seeing the frontier years as a galling time of hardship and privation, they evidently viewed them as a golden age which they very much wanted to retain. Thus, instead of moving further westward to find new lands, to build bustling towns, and to carve out snug farms, they sought to remain in their own beloved southern highlands, shutting themselves away from the rest of the world in order to avoid the advancing influences and restrictions of a civilization which they did not want. These essential differences in fundamental psychology, projected through a half-dozen or more intervening generations, account, at least partially, for the singular apartness from the rest of the nation the southern highlander maintains even today.

Anyone who knows the area and the people to whom I refer also knows that even now their pace of living is different, their values and outlook on life are different, and overall, they seem to be a happy and contented people. As long as they have enough to live on, acquired material wealth or possessions appears to be a priority considerably down from the top rung of the ladder, just as being able to do *what* they want to do *when* they want to do it, seems to be near the top rung of that ladder.

I write this material only after more than seven years of minute and specifically directed research; I write as well, from the vantage point of being born and reared in what some consider the declining phases of the culture which I have just described. Nevertheless, I believe that, as I relate the conditions of my early childhood and describe a recent visit to an area near my boyhood home, the reader will probably agree that remnants of the frontier culture still exist today and that some of its characteristics might be even stronger than they were in the days of my own youth.

B.   PERSONAL REFLECTIONS

I was born in the most remote and mountainous portion of East Tennessee just prior to the Great Depression, but as I grew to young manhood as one of five children I didn't even know that the country was experiencing hard times. To be sure, I learned early that life was rough and an uphill fight every inch of the way, but I knew no other way.

My parents' greatest pride was that "we lived on our own land and owed nothing to nobody." I was later to reflect that our own land consisted of about seventy acres so steep and poor as to be impractical to cultivate lest it wash away onto the narrow valley floor where about eight or ten acres of wild meadow provided the hay by which our livestock tolerated the long, harsh winters. Yet our family of seven flourished in the manner of our time by growing all our own food, making most of our clothing, growing and selling tobacco as the primary cash crop, and bartering chickens and eggs for the few necessities we could not take from the land, forest, and rivers. Eggs were worth about a penny each in trade, and a possum hide was worth fifteen or twenty cents, either at the nearest country store or from the "hide man" each spring.

We owned a pair of mules named Kate and Henry (Photo 16-B), we stacked our hay because we had no hay balers (photo 16-B), and much of the plowing was done with a bull tongue plow (photo 16-G).

We did own a wagon much like the one shown in photo 16-C, and the man shown unloading corn could very well be my father, whom we called "Pappie." Actually, most of the hauling was done by sled, because corn or hay was sledded off the steep hillsides where the wagon would not go.

The sled not only represented a method of transporting materials off steep hillsides, but also represented one of our most precious natural resources, wood. Although the sled shown in photo 16-E was made from sawed lumber, the ones which I remember best were made from young ash trees, grown with just the proper crook for good runners. My father would roam the forests for days looking for the correct ash trees from which to make sled runners. Then he would hew them *just so,* cut cross-member poles, and put the sled together with wooden pegs and wooden standards.

Wood was plentiful. It was used to build our log houses, to rive boards for roofs, to burn in our fireplaces for heat, to burn in our cook stoves for cooking; and from wood we carved *mauls* which we use to drive wooden wedges and wooden fence posts.

A good part of the late summer days, after crops were laid by, were utilized in cutting wood for the winter, cutting bushes from pasture land, patching the buildings, and getting prepared for winter.

Man's work and woman's work was rather arbitrarily divided, with a man's work being to labor in the fields (or to hunt and fish), and a woman's work being to keep the house chores done, mind the children, and tend the vegetable garden and crops near the house. It is seldom that one could find a man preparing the churning (as shown in photo 16-J), but it was quite common for a woman to have chores to do at night while the man of the house rested and smoked his pipe (as shown in photo 16-I).

A part of our *own land* included an old log house, log corn crib, and a rather new barn across the road. Old photographs of our house, reproduced so many times as to be of poor quality, appear in photos 16-S and 16-Z. My father and his four brothers and sisters, and his five children, were born in that same house, which had been passed on to my father, the youngest of his family. Actually, he had acquired it by buying the interests of his brothers and sisters, thereby owning all the old home place (about eighty acres). The same land had been his father's before him, ad infinitum, as far as my father knew, or at least cared to discuss. I recently bought the remains of the old log house and my youngest daughter (and her husband) moved and restored it. The log corn crib (photo 16-Y) was burned for firewood, not too many years ago, by some person who saw it as an item to be rid of, rather than a reminder of a golden past.

Our old log house had only two rooms, each about twenty-four feet square, and a fireplace in each room fed into the same chimney. But the living room had been partitioned to make a small bedroom in the end away from the fireplace. My two sisters slept in a cord bed in the kitchen, my parents slept in a second cord bed in the living room, and we three boys slept in the small partitioned room in beds our father had built from our own precious natural resource, wood.

I attended a one-room, one-teacher school, about a mile from our house. Today, I treasure a photograph (shown in 16-U) showing all five of my brothers and sisters attending that school at the same time. Presuming that there were minimum standard at that time, I suppose our school met them. There were no toilets except a *big rock* behind which the boys went, and hideaway below the hump where the girls disappeared (behind the bushes) for privacy.

Photographs that follow represent, in a very real sense, actual living and working conditions prevailing at the time and place of my rearing -- and they illustrate what I have been discussing. Although specific persons and places are sometimes mentioned, generally for identification/credit purposes, the primary intent is to depict generalities. As I have alluded to before, the TVA photographs were made by Lewis W. Hine about 1933 -- but some photographs are my own and some were donated by friends.

16A: Keck's General Store, Goin, Tennessee, 1936. Harry England and Otto Walker shopping for three 'possum hide's worth of candy and shotgun shells. Rebecca Keck, store attendant, was the author's wife's grandmother.

16-B: A farmer and his mules seen to be mutually admiring each other. Note hay stacked in background.

16-C: After the mules were fed, and maybe after supper, the farmer unloads his corn by hand.

16-D: An example of soil erosion—due to steepness, sparse ground cover, and non-use. The CCC stopped a great deal of this in the mid-to-late 1930s.

16-E: Boy, horse, and sled-load of corn just gathered from the field.

16-F: A typical "New Ground" just cleared, for planting in the spring. The farmer had to plow and hoe around the tree stumps—which was no easy task on such steep land.

16-G: Boy plowing with his mule and a bull-tongue plow. Most farm boys learned to plow as soon as they could reach the plow handles.

16-H: Wheat was cut by hand-cradle, tied in bundles and stacked—and each August the "thrashing machine" went from farm to farm, threshing the grain for a percentage of the crop.

16-I: **Man's work and woman's work was arbitrarily divided, by custom—but man's bandaged finger lent aid and support to his position as a mere observer. Note bed near the fireplace.**

16-J: Since man's work and woman's work was divided and specified by custom—and churning was woman's work—it must be assumed that this man had no wife.

16-K: Farmers had to inch further and further up the mountainside to find fields to cultivate.

16-L: "Boxed" house, with plenty of wood stacked for the winter. Such a house being wired for electricity was a rarity in the author's boyhood experience.

16-M: "Weather Boarded" house with stone chimney and "board" roof. It is likely that this is a log house, modernized with clap-board siding, as a sign of affluence.

16-N: Another "Boxed" house with stone chimney and board roof.

16-O: Self-sufficient homesite with its own water-driven grist mill.

16-P: A good, sturdy log cabin—in need of some repair.

16—Q:　Winter scene of "Boxed" house set back from roads—but then few had need for roads as such.

16-R: A view of a typical homesite in the author's boyhood experience.

16-S: Two-room log house in which the author's father and five brothers and sisters, and the author's five brothers and sisters, were born and reared. Author stands next to his father, who is leaning against the house.

16-T: A "Boxed" house, exactly like the one the author and his wife moved into as newlyweds in 1943.

16-U: Ridge School near Lone Mountain, Tennessee—about 1935—a one-teacher, one-room school. Author sits in front row, fifth from right, with his younger sister, Dora, to his right. Brother Clyde is third row back, second from right. Brother Edward is top row, center, with bib overalls, and sister, Georgia, is top left.

16-V: A typical one-room, one-teacher, school of the 1930s, in the author's experience.

16-W: Preparation for the following day's school work was done by the fireside, with father's encouragement.

16-X Author's brother. Clyde. and A-Model Ford. The family's
first automobile (about 1940).

16-Y: Left: author's mother and sister in front of log corn crib, about 1936.
        Right: author's father and mother, in Sunday dress, posing at edge of tobacco patch, about
        1940.

16-Z: The same log house as in Photograph 16-S, 1937 or 1938. Author is right rear. Photo also includes author's mother and father, two brothers and two sisters, two uncles, and an extra girl.

We were *average* people in the time and place where I was reared, in that most of our neighbors were owners of similar patches of steep land. They were subsistence farmers (as we were) and would often *trade out* work. Everyone generally made most of their tools and implements, and we used mules instead of horses. Living in a log house was not unusual, and certainly all the children I knew attended the same one-room school.

My parents insisted that all the children learn to read and write, for it was evident that we would need such knowledge in later life. After all, one must be able to *cipher* to prevent being cheated in bartering, and must be able to read so as to avoid embarrrassment from the neighbors.

Looking back, I can't remember, as a boy, being dissatisfied with my lot, or being anxious, unhappy, or even ambitious. I had everything I could want: plenty of food, adequate clothing, a warm house, and plenty of space in which to move around unmolested and unhampered. I was happy and free to roam the primitive forests hunting game for food, or walking in the woods simply to commune with nature.

There was a Missionary Baptist Church about two miles from our house, where a preacher held *services* one saturday and sunday each month. Usually I went to church on Sunday (Saturday was a work day), but most of the time I went only to visit with the boys in the church yard. Seldom did I go into the church house, nor did most of the other boys. We believed, we said, that church was only for girls and old folks.

I confess, however, that I did sometimes listen through the open window. I especially remember listening to the singing and wondering how the old folks remembered the tunes to the mournful songs. The hymn books were about three by five inches in size, and they contained only words, like poems, with no music. I had heard that some churches even had musical instruments which were played as accompaniment to the singing.

We lived more than twenty miles from the nearest town, the county seat, which had a population of about five hundred I suppose. I don't remember how often my father went to town (about twice a year, I guess, to trade), but I do definitely remember my first trip. I was eleven years old when I won a spelling match at school, and as a prize, my teacher took me to see a movie. That movie was "The China Clipper," and that was the beginning of an awakening to the fact that there was a larger world -- and that I was growing up in a time, place, and manner apart from that larger world. It was not to sink home completely, however, just how far from the rest of the nation the southern highlander really was and how intervening generations had made us different, until many years later when I had the opportunity to research the subject at some length.

In my youth, in the mid to late 1930's, U.S. Highway 25-E, a two-laned, dirt road ran about three and one-half miles from our house. Country roads were often impassable for automobiles, but then no one of my acquaintance had an automobile, anyway, and the roads were good enough for horse-and-wagon traveling.

We had no electricity; firelight and kerosene (coal oil) lamp provided the light by which we read and studied. At least for us, there was no such thing as a daily newspaper; school books were simple and rather scarce—especially so since there was no free textbook program. That meant, of course, that we bought each book from the "chicken and egg" money.

The wood-burning fireplaces provided the heat for our log house, and the job of cutting wood was a year-around chore if we didn't stack away enough every August, because, as indicated previously, the cookstove also burned wood. We took a great deal of our food from the forests and rivers, and the issue was not obtaining it but the storing and caring for it until used. Meat was generally cured by salting or drying; glass canning jars were scarce, even if one could afford to buy them. Corn and tobacco were the main crops that we grew; corn was our principal food crop and tobacco our chief cash crop.

An eighth-grade education was considered excellent for that time and place, but after seeing "The China Clipper," and reading some books that an affluent aunt had given me, I was unknowingly being awakened from generations of "apartness." Therefore, my immediate older brother and I decided to go to high school and see what it was like. My parents said it was all right to go, they reckoned, if we would buy our own books and clothes, and keep our share of the chores and fieldwork done. (That brother is now a doctor of veterinary medicine.) The high school was about twenty miles away; and the nearest that the school bus came to our farm was three-and-one-half miles. In the winter months I got out of bed at 5:00 A.M., built a fire in each fireplace and in the cookstove, then called my oldest sister to prepare breakfast. The livestock, which usually consisted of a team of mules, two or three cows, and three or four hogs, were fed before breakfast. Then the three-and-one-half-mile walk began that took just over an hour, usually from 6:30 to 7:30 A.M. to catch the school bus. In the afternoon the same distance was retraced on the return home. On a few rare occasions I missed the school bus and was thereby forced to walk the twenty miles to or from school.

During my four years of high school I became further awakened to the fact that I was probably decended from American pioneer stock who had settled and lived in the southern highlands since the early 1700s, and who, generation after generation, had remained in the deep hollows and remote, narrow valleys in order to avoid the advancing influences and restrictions of civilization. As I studied and reflected I became increasingly aware of the evidence that my parents were still living much as their ancestors had lived one-hundred-fifty or two-hundred years before them, and that their primary store of knowledge was what their parents had showed and told them. Because of their great love for freedom, to do as they chose whenever they chose, and their resolve to avoid organized and *new* ways, they viewed their galling time of hardship and privation as a golden age which they wanted to retain. Because they saw no reason for change, they remained largely like their ancestors before them—and their ancestors before them.

In my first year of school I completed the primer, first grade, and second grade; since I completed one regular grade each year thereafter, I was somewhat ahead of most of my age group. My high school was a small, rural one where the study of agriculture by the boys and home economics by the girls was the latest in curriculum planning of the New Deal era. I vividly remember learning about cover crops, hybrid seed, and the use of chemical fertilizers; I happily passed that knowledge on to my father and tried to put it into practice myself. For the most part, however, he farmed his *own land* the way he always had, the way his father had taught him, until the day he died in 1962.

My high school class had about forty graduates, and in preparation for graduation I don't remember any counselling or advising about higher education or vocational/industrial training. As I view it now, it seems that even the teachers assumed that none of their graduates would, or could, do anything but continue in the ways of their hillbilly ancestors. I remember broaching the idea to my parents and some of my teachers that I thought I would like to go to college: I had heard that in Berea, Kentucky, there was a college where one could work his way completely through if he were smart enough and strong enough. Although always small, I was wiry, and academically I was third in my high school class. Nevertheless, I was told very quickly by both parents and teachers that I was neither strong enough nor smart enough; besides, I hadn't the remotest prospect of the small amount of cash I would need. Therefore, when I completed high school within a few days of my seventeenth birthday, I did what my parents and teachers expected of me: I settled in to help around the farm.

In my third year of high school I had met a young lady who attended the junior high school just down the hill, and even though she was just approaching fifteen and I, sixteen, we very quickly developed a special feeling for each other. In spite of our youth, however, or perhaps because of it, I soon realized that I had fallen in love with her at the very beginning of our acquaintance, and I never seriously considered *courting* anyone else thereafter. From time to time I briefly flirted with some of my female cousins (who my sweetheart didn't know were by cousins) just to get my real sweetheart's attention. I knew from the beginning, however, that someday we would be married. Sure enough, in her sixteenth and my seventeenth year, we were married.

My father-in-law was a school teacher, and had served two terms in county court as a squire. My wife's entire family was much more affluent, in material goods and more accustomed to the ways of the outside world, than my family. They were greatly opposed to our marriage, not because of me, they said, but because of our ages. My family didn't seem to care one way or the other, as I recall, and made no comment. I could write a great deal about our pros and cons of teen-age marriages, about whether or not we were ready emotionally and financially, etcetera. In the final analysis, however, I would conclude, as I have many times, that we should have married when we did, and I remain as convinced today as I was then that our marriage was and is right.

I had no money, no income, and even owed a few hundred dollars as a result of part ownership of an old automobile which was by then wrecked and gone, but my wife had a cow as part of her dowry. We stayed with my parents a few months before moving into a three-room "boxed" house belonging to my wife's aunt and uncle, to whom we paid two dollars each month rent, including pasture for our cow. I got a job as handy-man around a small lead and zinc mine at thirty-five cents per hour; I sometimes took home seventeen dollars a week.

Those were the glorious days when we walked hand-in-hand just down the road to milk the cow; when we made love in the chicken house and got chicken mites on us; when we talked far into the nights about our dreams of tomorrow, and then made love into the wee hours of the morning as if to confirm the ideas and make them binding. We learned to face each day and each obstacle with declarations of our love for each, and to voice the words of love and respect for each other for all the days of our lives, no matter what they might bring. Forty-nine years later, and with the same beautiful girl by my side as my wife, we can vividly remember the glorious days of our youth, but we don't necessarily regard them as the *good old days*. We feel that we are now living in the very midst of the *good new days*, for which glorious early days set the pattern. And both of us are still very much convinced that the future might hold even better *good old days* for us.

In the first months of our marriage we bought an A-Model Ford, with a rumble seat, with a promise to pay later. Incidentally, it did not run. Many head-gaskets and countless push-offs later, we finally discovered a cracked engine block, which was the reason we got for almost nothing in the first place. That was a venture that cost us our cow, but it was a lesson that had to be learned.

About that same time we were having both our families for Sunday dinner; so on Saturday night I had caught our only hen and fastened her in the barn, in preparation for slaughtering her for our Sunday dinner. When I went to fetch the hen she couldn't found, but eventually was discovered drowned in a cistern in the barn. Without the chicken there would be no Sunday dinner, for we had nothing else to cook; so I plucked and cleaned the drowned hen and my wife cooked her with wonderfully thin dumplings that almost melted in one's mouth. No one present had ever eaten any better chicken and dumplings, they declared. Not surprisingly, the secret of the wet hen was not revealed until many years thereafter.

My wife was just over six months pregnant when I was drafted into the army in the latter part of World War II and sent to Florida to undergo infantry training. There my experiences and associations with young men from many distant parts of the nation and many walks of life added to my awakening realization that time had bypassed the way of life still followed by many in the southern highlands. New friends from the larger cities of the northern part of the United States poked fun at my way of talking and my lack of knowledge about most things outside my limited experiences in the southern highlands. However much they ridiculed my accent, the words I used, and my unworldliness they soon learned to have great respect for my ingenuity in making do with the materials at hand, my ability to read the weather, and my communion with the land, forest, and animals. I remember, for example, that in learning how to find directions by compass readings I discovered that the course was a lopsided octagon with seven turning points. We were instructed to follow the compass readings and distance instructions, visit each station or turning point, leaving a note at each to prove that we had been there, and report back to the starting point as soon as possible; the winning team of ten men would be rewarded with a truck ride back to camp; and the losers would walk. The catch was that it was dark, and the course crossed and re-crossed a stream many times. The stream was shallow and wadable at first, but probably deeper and not wadable further on. In addition to finding our way to each check-point, we had to figure out how to get across the stream. I persuaded the others of my team that more than likely the stream split the course, with four stations on one side and three on the other. So we prepared duplicate notes and searched for the first station. Half the team waded the stream and set out to find the stations on one side,while I and the other half of the team set out to find the stations on our side of the stream; leaving notes at each station. When the team was once again together, sure enough each had found three stations - and combined with the first station we had found together, that made seven. My team never understood how I was able to navigate the course backwards and find the stations in the dark. Although I had actually navigated partly from instinct and partly from a recalculation of compass readings, I did not reveal to the others how I had accomplished it. Nevertheless, we were far ahead of the others in completing the course, sitting calmly in our dry tent when they returned. Later we rode back to camp in a six-by-six, and the remainder of the company walked.

In spite of the fact that I was one of the smallest men, in physical stature, of the two hundred men in my company, our commander made me trainee leader.

As a result, it was my lot to march beside the company commander; whether or not he was present, I set the pace of march. At the end of seventeen weeks of basic training we bivouacked for two weeks, capping off the period with a thirty-mile hike back to camp; it lasted from 12:01 A.M. to 8 A.M. Almost half the men dropped out before we reached our destination. I made it in fine shape, showered, shaved, and headed for Jacksonville to meet my wife and five-week-old son who were arriving at noon that day; then we walked the streets of Jacksonville all Saturday afternoon looking for an apartment, or even a room, for rent.

Very late in World War II I was sent to Europe to join an infantry division made up mostly of men from Pennsylvania and New York. There I was once again confronted with the many differences in heritage, habits, and upbringing between us. In addition to being products of diverse ways of life in the United States, many of my new friends were only one generation removed from current European habits.

My military unit was engaged in combat against the German forces for the last five months of World War II; much of our time was spent in the mountains where we had to forage off the land. Here again my hillbilly know-how of making-do with the materials at hand served me and my comrades well enough that we hardly noticed that our kitchen truck appeared only about once or twice each week. Typically, in our daily moving, we stopped, dug foxholes, looked for food, ate, then rested. We never knew how long we would stay in one spot; one day I dug seventeen fox-holes.

Early one afternoon, after we had stopped and dug in, I found a goose and a turkey lurking in the area. While others searched for pots in which to boil them, I built a fire and kept a watchful eye on the food on foot. Just as two of the men returned with pots and I had a good fire going, the order came to move out. Since I obviously couldn't carry both birds, I quickly decided on the goose instead of the turkey, bound his feet, taped his bill with a Bandaid—borrowed from the medic—to prevent his biting, tied him to my pack, and we moved out. Someone else carried the·boiling pot, and when we stopped again we repeated the fire routine. It took three stops to get the goose killed, cleaned, and cooked, but needless to say we didn't go hungry that night.

After World War II ended in Europe I remained in Germany about three months, and as I watched the German people reorganize their lives and the communities and societies around them, I was impressed once again with how little I understood the ways of organized society outside the southern highland. I watched as they reestablished family and community contacts, as they sought law and order and the right to govern themselves, as they searched to share their ideas with others around them, and as they obviously yearned for and sought better ways to do things. It was apparent that they wanted to be part of something, to lend themselves and their ideas to building something better, whereas I had sprung from a culture that wanted to be separated from something. Probably that was the final step in my awakening to the differences and apartness of my cultural background from the more progressive parts of the world. Also formulated at that time was the first conscious desire to learn why I and my heritage were so different.

In the next few months, after the war with Japan had ended and I heard some talk about a GI Bill, I began to believe and hope, for the first time, that I perhaps could go to college. Maybe I could learn something of what so many other people already seemed to know, or at least ascertain how to go about learning further on my own. I was aware, even then, that, if I were to be at all successful in obtaining the three greatest ambitions of my life, my first task would be learning how to discover and recognize knowledge. I did a lot of thinking, in those last few months of 1945, about what I wanted out of life, and I came to a fairly definite conclusion. My first ambition was to become educated to the point of getting a better job, which would provide for my family a different and better existence than mine and that of my ancestors. Second, I wanted to learn about the history (and perhaps the future) of the world, about how society came to be organized as it is; having learned, I wanted to become a part of it. Third, I had an overwhelming desire to investigate the heritage of the southern highlander, perhaps learning something of my own background at the same time.

In January 1946 I entered college on the GI Bill with $90 per month for the subsistence of myself, wife, and two children (a second child had been born in August 1945, and a third would arrive in October 1948). Even though I worked the maximum time I could spare from my studies and enrolled in advanced ROTC mostly for the money, those were the lean years. They were, however, an important part of an overall twenty-five-year period of striving toward the first and second of my three major goals. I earned a bachelor's degree, a teacher's certificate, and was commissioned a second lieutenant in the Air Force. After starving through one year of teaching high school on a $1500 annual state salary, in 1950 I decided to return to military life. As a second lieutenant with seven years' longevity my pay was good, and with hard work and considerable luck I earned regular promotions, thereby keeping my family relatively free from financial worries for the following twenty-one years. Because we traveled a great deal, we met and lived with people from many walks of life in many different geographical locations. However, as Will Rogers reportedly said "I never met a man I didn't like," I can honestly say that we never have lived anywhere that I didn't like and enjoy, and I never have met a person from whom I didn't learn something. I don't think that any other profession could have afforded me the opportunity of learning as much about people and places as did the Air Force.

During my years in service I earned a master's

degree in education and a master of science degree in management. At the age of forty-four I was fairly well satisfied with my progress toward the first two of my three major goals. Therefore, as I continued to work toward a refinement of those goals, I retired from the Air Force in order to seek further training and prepare for the research and systematic study necessary to realize my third goal; i.e. a better knowledge of the southern highlander and his heritage, and perhaps some understanding of my own background and ancestral lineage. Thus, I came to the University of Tennessee for a three-year administrative assignment, after which I completed my doctorate. Simultaneously, I began the researching, documenting, and interviewing necessary for the information and the story that follows in Parts 2 and 3.

I was amazed and a little overwhelmed at the massiveness of the data which I was able to accumulate in very short order. As I continued to gather, organize, and rewrite material, I very quickly realized that I could place all of it in five very distinct categories: (1) a stereotyped or sanitized view of the southern highlander or hillbilly, (2) remembrances of what it was like to grow up in the southern highlands in the 1930's, (3) notes on a revisit to a geographic location near where I was reared some fifty odd years ago, (4) a plausible version of Jamie's travels from London to Appalachia, and (5) historical perspectives, based on a solid review of medieval history, concerning what probably caused the great migration to the southern highlands at the time and in the manner it occurred. As previously noted on page 3, the fifth category will not be treated in depth in this book.

Part 2

For Old-Time's Sake

FOR OLD-TIME'S SAKE

As I have previously indicated, anyone who knows the area and the people of whom I write also knows that their pace of living is different, their values and outlook on life are different, and as a group they seem to be a very happy and contented people. The two dominating criteria that guide most of their actions are (1) to keep the peace and serenity of the old ways in order to enjoy a quiet and simple life, and (2) to be able to do what they want to do when they want to do it.

The following photographs depict the serenity of typical country scenes found in many parts of the southern highlands even today— places one sometimes has to lay down a fence-gap in the road in order to proceed up the road; where cane is still grown, the juice pressed out, and boiled down until it becomes molasses; and where many old log houses and barns still stand occupied.

In the summer of 1976 I drove into a remote mountainous region less than fifty miles from Knoxville, Tennessee, for the specific purpose of visiting a family of whom I had heard my mother speak many times.

Over the years she had told many stories about a man named Mr. Bull, a grown man when she was yet a girl, and how he professed to know more than anyone else about the early pioneer days of that region. I had known of that "holler" for many years, and knew that a great many of the inhabitants still lived as their ancestors did one hundred and fifty years or more ago. What prompted my visit at that particular time was an article in the Knoxville News-Sentinel, Sunday, July 11, 1976, reading essentially as follows: "Representative John Duncan announced that the Powell valley REA, serving parts of Union and Claiborne counties in Tennessee, received a loan of $2,430,000 to help finance electrical services, including fifty-four miles of distribution lines, to an additional 1,000 customers who have heretofore never had electrical power available to them."

I knew that Mr. Bull, now probably in his nineties, was one of the "1,000 customers" who, even in 1976, had never had electricity in his home. I wanted to get his reaction to that, in addition to getting more firsthand information about other things concerning which I was writing.

When I turned up the holler toward Mr. Bull's house a ten-or eleven-year-old boy was squatted on the bank of the road near a mailbox; he advised me to park my car there, because I couldn't drive all the way, and further up there was no place to turn around. I followed his advice, and after commissioning him, for a quarter, to keep an eye on my car, I set off to walk

36-A: Current rural scenes like this one are common-place in "our parts."

36-B: This is like going back home.

36-C: Although not a typical current scene, the author can take you to places similar, within forty miles of Knoxville, Tennessee.

36-D: Similarities to Mr. Bull's house.

36-E: If the dress code did not betray this scene, the author would attest to seeing this a few weeks ago.

36-F: Many houses similar to this one are still in use.

36-G: This "Cane Mill" still exists and operates every year (or at least one like it).

36-H: The juice is pressed from the cane as it passes between two rollers.

36-I: The cane juice is poured into a vat and boiled until it thickens into sorghum molasses.

36-J: Many log barns similar to this one are still in use today.

36-K: Is this woman admiring her newly installed electrical service?

36-L: Another not uncommon homestead in use today.

the approximate mile to Mr. Bull's house. The road was a rough, steep trail that had been worn into the side of the mountain over the years by horses and wagons. Three times within that mile the road crossed an unbridged stream, but for the foot travelers there were rocks or logs on which to cross without getting their feet wet.

As I approached the part-frame, part-log house that seemed to protrude meekly from a wooded area at the end of the road, I saw a young woman, apparently in her early twenties, snatch what was likely her baby from the porch floor and disappear into the house. An old man with about a week-old stubble of beard sat on a split-bottomed chair. The chair rested only on its two back legs, because the old man was leaning back against a porch support, handy to the edge so he could spit his tobacco juice on the ground. He appeared to be concentrating on a red cedar whittling stick, but as I approached he said, without even looking up, "Come in, mister, and sit a spell. You are a stranger in these parts ain't yuh?"

I took the proffered chair which he pushed forward with his foot, told him who I was, that my mother was a Howerton and that she had been born somewhere near here in 1888. Then I asked if he was Mr. Bull and if he remembered my mother's family.

"Reckon I do," he said. "I am Lige Bull and I was bornd in this here house in 1880. They wuz four girls and two boys in the *Haunten* family as I recollect. But I wuz sweet on the oldest girl anyway. Her name was Laurie. Wuz that your Ma?''

I told him that it was indeed my mother, but that she had been dead five years then, and only one member of her family was still living. That seemed to set him off to musing again.

"I alles thought your Ma was part Cherokee," he said, " 'cause she wusn't like her brothers and sisters. I'm part Indian, you know. My pappie was part Cherokee, a quarter I guess, 'cause I remember him telling me that his Ma wuz half Cherokee. That would a been my Granny. Best I recollect from Pappie's stories my great-grand pappie must a found him a Cherokee wife and settled in this here same house in 1825, I think it wuz. He married three times and had twenty-one children in all—and I'm the youngest and only one still living—and I'm ninety-six-year-old come next week."

I needed to keep him talking if possible, but I knew better than to let him think I was pumping him for information; so I tilted my chair back against the porch post like Mr. Bull and said, "This is about the most quiet and peaceful place I have ever seen."

"Ain't it the truth?" Uncle Lige said. "Not a neighbor within a mile, and just the three of us lives in this old house. I can remember, though, when this old house wuz a-jumping with a dozen or more kids—and the patches wuz all tended and everbody had work to do. That's the ruination of young people to-day—they don't work. They piddle at this and piddle at that, and don't work up a good sweat in a year."

I agreed that times were changing rapidly, and that even during my lifetime, which was barely more than half his, what was considered good or bad, as far as work was concerned, and a definition of the real necessities of life were things that were undergoing tremendous change. I told him that my mother, then my four brothers and sisters and I, had grown up just over the ridge much as he and his children had, but that in later years I had been privileged to travel all over the world. I knew that Uncle Lige was a simple man, from the standpoint of worldly knowledge, but I also realized that he was quick and sharp, of mature intelligence and juman judgment, and that if I were unable to convince him of my sincerity, honesty, and basic earthiness he wouldn't continue the conversation he had begun. Therefore, I watched closely to discern what he was thinking of me and what I was saying. The air was strangely quiet for many seconds before Uncle Lige rocked forward to set his chair on all four legs. Then he peered at me, with one eye squinting as if he was seeing me for the first time.

"You mean to tell me that you have lived in them there big cities and even across the waters? Some of my grand-younguns and great-grand younguns tell me that there are places where people live in 'partment houses and they is thick as squirrels in hicker-nut time—and they can never get out of them places. Why, they tell me that they's so many people in some places that the giverment has to give them somethin' to eat."

I told Uncle Lige that a lot of that was true, but I believed there was only one basic difference in people; no matter where they lived or had grown up, or what they believed in or were accustomed to. Most people's efforts, I declared, in all parts of the world, are directed toward making a better world for their children than it had been for them. I paused to see how Uncle Lige was responding.

"I guess that's right," he said. "Now jest take me. I wuz borned and raised right here in this house. My pappie learnt me how to make a living tending patches and huntin. And he alles told me to git beholden to nobody. I guess he told me a thousand times to mind my own business in this world - and if I didn't need any help to mind mine, then nobody didn't need any to mind thern either."

I simple nodded and rocked my chair modestly, as he continued. I had to encourage him to continue talking. And he did.

"Some of my brothers and sisters lived clost around here," he said, "and some of 'em moved off. I guess they's all dead but me, leastwise as far as I know. But I alles wanted to stay right here. I've not been as fer as Knoxville but twist in my life, and then I couldn't wait to git back home. But then I know I'm funny. I put great store in doin jest what I want to do and when I want to do it - and nobody can't tell me different. I ain't got much, but then I don't need much anyway. I've got a cow and a mule, and good patches growing, and I've even some good 'backer' for what little money I need. My great grand-youngun, Marthie, lives with me, and she reads the Bible to me ever day of the world.''

I gingerly approached the subject of the REA bringing electricity through these parts of his mountains and asked what he thought about it. (I had noticed that he had no electrical wiring attached to his house.

'Don't matter much to me,'' he said. Didn't sign up for it 'cause I reckon I don't need it. Some people tell me that all I got to do is have my house ward, and then just turning a little knob will make light. And they talk about 'letric iceboxes and freezing things. But reckon I'll just keep my coal-oil lamp and lantern—they ain't worn out yet. But mind you I've got the money to do it if I wanted to.''

We talked on for the better part of two hours, with Uncle Lige doing most of the talking. He told me that he reckoned that life had been good to him, giving him two wives and seven children, ''and most of them was right out there in that little graveyard.'' He had always been able to do just what he wanted to, he said, and he allowed ''a body couldn't ask for much more from life than that.'' I agreed, as I arose to leave, telling him that I would be back soon to sit and talk if that was all right with him. He allowed that I was more than welcome to come back and see him any time I had a good notion to.

When I had retraced the mile to the main road I found my automobile where I had left it, but the boy was gone, or at least he wasn't visible. Everything was all right, however, since rocks had been placed behind each wheel to keep the car from rolling. As I began the drive home I reflected, as I had many times, on the wonder of such men as Uncle Lige Bull and such a frontier situation as I had just witnessed; there was little doubt in my mind they were the spawning ground for many of our currrent mores and values. I thought of how the frontier situation in the southern highlands had produced men and women who remained in the mountains simply because they wanted to, and I asked if Uncle Lige Bull represented the people who had let life pass them by.   How happy was Uncle Lige Bull, in comparison to the thousands of other people I knew who were considered more worldly? I had to admit that, in the final analysis, Uncle Lige appeared to be as happy and contented a man as I had ever seen.

As I continued on my way home, still reflecting on my visit, I recalled the following words and ideas I had recently come across in *The Southern Appalachian Heritage*, with which I agree, since they state my own philosophy:

> In their search for freedom and a place of their own, the first white settlers of the Southern Appalachians entered a primeval wilderness of unparalled beauty and resources, a land of soaring peaks, turbulent streams, dense forests, and abundant wildlife. But nature had provided the Appalachians with subtle methods of controlling determined intruders. Once entered, the rugged, remote wilderness closed behind the frontiersman, cutting him off from the rest of the world.
>
> The fertile coves and valleys were small and often

far apart; their boundaries would not extend to make room for the growing stream of people hoping to carve their homes in the wilderness. As a result, the pioneers who followed the first settlers pushed further west, leaving behind the inhabitants of the mountains in their secluded world, isolated from their compatriots beyond the mountains and from each other.

They were so isolated as to be out of the mainstream of civilization, and their very existence was forgotten by the rest of the country. Their way of life changed so little through the years that they became a separate people with their own character, customs, and dialect. For most of two centuries time stood still for the southern high-lander.[1]

And yet, I marveled, while some of the Uncle Liges of the southern highlands had crept further back into the hills and had remained there simply because they wanted to, that same frontier situation had spawned such great American scouts and leaders as Daniel Boone, Kit Carson, Sam Bowie, and others who, in buckskin jacket and with butcher knife, tomahawk, and rifle had marked the trail for a century of westward migration. One of the most noteworthy facts of that phenomenon, however, is that few of them took to the trail for life, but rather most of them eventually returned to the mountains that had produced them.

[1]Herma Cate, Clyde Ussery, and Randy Armstrong, *The Southern Appalachian Heritage* (Kingsport, Tenn.: The Holston Publishing Co., 1974), p. 12.

Harry M. Caudill spoke of the southern highlander as follows:

> It is unlikely that history will ever again record the appearance of a man who, as a type, will possess the hardihood, the sturdy self-reliance, and the fierce independence of the American frontiersman in the forty years preceding the turn of the century, and in the next decade or two thereafter. He was an uncouth brawler, wholly undisciplined and untamed, and it was practically impossible to direct or control his energies in any sustained undertaking. But when the objectives were within his grasp and were approved by him, the frontiersman multiplied by any considerable number constituted a well-nigh irresistible force on the North American ntinent.[2]

Also, in my reverie, I realized that I was mulling over some of Kephart's ideas. When he was writing about the southern highlander, about 1912, he indicated that some missionaries were shocked and scandalized by what seemed to be an incurable perversity and race degeneration, but that in his opinion it was nothing of the sort. There is good reason for what we find as method and practice in the "hills," and most of what we see is the result of isolation and the lack of opportunity. It is no more hopeless, he explained, than the same features of life in the Scotland of two centuries ago. Kephart did go ahead to say that, in

[2] Harry M. Caudill, *Night Comes to the Cumberlands* (Boston: Little, Brown & Co.), p. 12.

his opinion, the future of the hillbilly was a basic economic problem which should be studied hand-in-hand with the educational problem, and that it is likely that civilization repels the mountaineer only until he is shown something to be gained from it, i.e. something that he has sought or is looking for to make his life, and that of his family, better.

In summary, these works of Kephart form a fitting conclusion to this part of *Appalachian Haven:*

> But even in writing with some severe restraints it will be necessary at times to show conditions so rude and antiquated that professional apologists will growl, and others may find my statements hard to credit as typical of anything in our modern America. So let me remind the reader again that a full three-fourths of our mountaineers still live in the eighteenth century, and that in their farflung wilderness, away from large rivers and railways, the habits, customs, and morals of the people have changed little from those of our colonial frontier. [3]

[3]Horace Kephart, *Our Southern Highlanders* (Knoxville: The University of Tennessee Press, 1976). p. 285.

Part 3
Jamie's Story

INTRODUCTION

An introduction to Part 3 is, by necessity, a summary of Parts 1 and 2 and a logical reason for leaping headlong into part 3, and is thusly explained: Having taken a stereotyped view of the southern highlander, recalled and recorded how I grew up in that culture some fifty years ago, and having recorded a visit to a similar geographic area in 1976, confirming that even today some of the inhabitants still live much as their ancestors did one hundred fifty or two hundred years ago, I found that I was more curious than ever about the personal lives of the early inhabitants of the southern highlands. I found myself thinking of those early Americans not merely as mythical frontiersmen, but as real live people (maybe even my own ancestors) with real hopes, and joys, and aspirations.

More than six years of minute, detailed, and persistent research went into the development of Part 3 because I insisted that it be not only humanistic and believable but also historically accurate. Therefore, after gathering the data and information from records, writings, and interviews, I developed what I believe to be a logical, reasonable, and plausible story of the coming of the first white settlers to southern Appalachia. Jamie's story presents the humanistic side of the reasons for the migration to the southern highlands. I have written this account because, in my research, I found a great deal of information about the southern highlander's distinctive lifestyle as well as the reasons for it, but I found no story such as I have written about specific persons who actually did migrate in the early 1700's.

Part 3 is presented as a story developed from facts and historical documentation, and it is authenticated by footnotes and appendixes. The facts are there, and no mistaking that, even though I have permitted myself a writer's license of romanticizing this historical account simply for the purpose of making it more readable and enjoyable. Almost as an afterthought, I find myself thinking, "These could have been my ancestors."

A.   JAMIE IN LONDON ABOUT 1728

On a cold, dark February night in the year 1728, an old, retired professor of history and theology, a man of great learning was summoned from his bed to come to St. Katherine's "boarding depot," near the Tower of London, to attend an outbreak of fever. Although he was not a doctor of medicine, he was called Doc Bling, and it was well known in some circles that he had considerable practical medical knowledge which he gave of freely when requested. Often he was the only knowledgeable person available who could and would give advice and not expect payment. A man in his seventies who considered himself a student and practioner of humanism, James George Bling, had earned an academic doctorate from an Austrian University.   He had taught, studied, and researched in four major universities in western Europe, but his last active years had been spent at St. Peter's College in London, commonly called Westminister School, where he had worked diligently for the acceptance and establishment of public education for all children. His ideas were far ahead of their time, and he had given up his teaching with a heavy heart, not having convinced the authorities that education for all children was practical or needed. He lived alone now, in a basement flat, since his wife had died twelve years earlier. Previous to his wife's death, however, they had acquired and saved enough to keep body and soul together without having to work every day; thus he was able to carry on his beloved reading, human research, and occasional lecturing to small groups concerning the history of mankind and its ultimate destiny. Because he was particularly drawn to the downtrodden, the lame, the paupers, and the prisioners, in recent years he had utilized every opportunity to give of himself to those groups in hope both, that he could learn more about them and that at the same time perhaps he could assist them with his knowledge and philosophy. He had no children and no family, but all who knew him recognized his passion and sympathy for those less fortunate than himself. For his labors and advice he asked nothing except the opportunity to serve people, especially to encourage them to think for themselves rather than to allow themselves to be herded about and treated like animals.

As he moved slowly along the streets near St. Paul's Cathedral, he heard groans and whimpers of apparently human origin coming from beneath a pile of rubble. When he stopped shuffling his feet the noises stopped, but when he moved forward again, the whimpering resumed. Doc Bling started and stopped four or five times as he tried to decide whether he should offer assistance, but remembering the mission he was on, he made a mental note to return home this way. Perhaps he could find who was causing the noises and attend that person's needs.

Upon his arrival at the service entrance of St. Katherine's, he was taken into a dungeonlike room filled with fifty or sixty men, varying in age from about twelve to seventy years. The stench was almost unbearabale and the smell of fever was everywhere. The man who had opened the door for Doc gestured toward the dozen or more ovbiously very sick men who were huddled together in one corner of the room, asking what could be done for them. Doc wanted to remind the man that he was not a physician, but that in his opinion separation of the ill from the well men, getting some ventilation into the room and feeding them some decent food would probably do a great deal. However, he knew that such suggestions not only would not be heeded, but if he voiced them he would not be asked or permitted to return; so he gave the man some healing powders to mix with their food and said he would return in a day or so after he had studied the matter and prepared some remedies.

That was not Doc Bling's first visit to the boarding depot which served as a virtual prison for keeping people a month or more until the master of some ship could transport them to America, where they would serve as indentured servants, redemptioners, or as Christian servants. Among them were rogues, vagabonds, convicts, and human rabble of all description,

as well as kidnapped children raked from the gutter
or bought out of debtor's prison only to be sold into
white slavery. Some were unfortunate French, German , and Swiss protestants fleeing religious persecu-
tion; some were starving, unhappy Irish or rack-
rented Scottish farmers, and some were poverty-
stricken peasants and artisans of all sorts. It was a
well known fact people of every age and kind were
decoyed, deceived, seduced, spirited, inveigled, or for-
cibly kidnapped and carried as servants to serve plantation owners in the American colonies. But many of
them went willingly, because it was a last resort for
scoundrels, or perhaps they simply wanted to get out
of their own country for some reason. Some were ordinary individuals of decent substance, and a few were
entitled by custom of the time to be call gentlemen.
But all would share the same destiny; that is, they
would become bond servants for four or more years
to whatever colonial master that could buy them.

Doc Bling had just visited St. Katherine's (as he
had the Lord only knows how many times), which
was one of the many depots around London where
such human cargo was kept until passage to the New
World could be arranged. The major cause of the
wretched conditions Doc Bling had just witnessed was
that, since the endeavor was profit motivated, these
unfortunate people were at the mercy of the entrepre-
neur who had bought them out of prison, or had
otherwise made an offer, promisee, or contract to take
them to America and a better life; thus, any funds

spent on food, lodging, and medicine diminished that profit.

With these things weighing heavily on his mind, and knowing that there was precious little that he, as one person, could do about them, Doc Bling retraced his steps to the alley behind St. Paul's Cathedral where he had heard the groaning and whimpering. As he approached a pile of boxes and rags he heard a wheezing sound, and he began to remove some of the litter to see what was there. As he removed the last of the pile, he could see a child of perhaps nine or ten years cowering with upflung arms, as if to ward off expected blows to the head. Doc spoke slowly, softly, yet firmly, as he told the child to stand where he could be seen. The child, now in crouching position, with head bowed, did not move or answer. It occured to Doc that most likely the child was ill and perhaps could not move.

Little by little Doc got the child to his feet, but he remained in a crouching position, as if his midsection might break if he straightened up. He was wrapped in the tattered remains of a greatcoat, and his feet and lower legs were tied in burlap or something like hemp strings. As Doc spoke encouragingly, urging the child to follow him, the youth never spoke; seemingly he barely could stand alone. The feeling did not escape the old man that, had the child been well, he already most surely either would have attacked him or run away; certainly he would not be a willing victim of any proffered assistance. However, as the case was,

Doc knew that he must get the child to his feet and to some place where he could determine whether there was any aid he could render. Therefore he half-carried, half-dragged the child the quarter-mile to his flat, and, more or less exhausted, dropped him in a corner.

When the tapers were lighted and the grate stoked up a bit—and when Doc himself had had time to catch his breath—he began unwrapping the child to determine what, if anything, could be done. The boy, still cowering and never speaking, grudgingly gave up each piece of tattered cloth and string from his body, and, as the warmth of the room seeped in, he began to cough excessively. As Doc continued to unwind the tattered clothing, he soon discovered a boy eight, nine, or perhaps even ten years old, with emaciated body displaying dozens of bruises and open sores. Apparently the child's lungs were in deplorable condition, evidenced by his obvious difficulty in breathing. Doc kept up a continual monologue as he gave the child some wheat porridge, wrapped him in a comforter near the grate, and placed an unguent under his nose to assist his breathing. Nothing more could be done, he thought, for surely the child needed sleep and rest more than anything else.

From Doc's own bed, not much more than a straw mat in a corner near the fire, he could hear the boy thrashing about and moaning in his sleep as the night wore on. A half-dozen times or more he pulled the comforter up around the boy, and each time he detected a worsening fever and a horrible odor pervading the child's body. By dawn Doc was convinced that the boy was afflicted with some serious desease, and he knew that he would have to ask his physician friend for advice and medicine. While he was there, he thought, he also would report the fever in St. Katherine's and request the physician's advice about it.

As the bleak dawn barely lighted the flat, Doc tried to rouse the child to take food. He could get only a mild stare and blinking of the eyes from the boy, however, but at least he no longer cowered and shrank away. Perhaps he was too weak even for that, for Doc could not persuade the boy to show any interest in either food or water. As he stoked the grate slowly and prepared to brave the bleak February morning cold, the thought came to Doc that perhaps the boy was deranged; worse yet, maybe he had the plague. Although Doc had never experienced the plague, he had read a great deal about it. In any case, he must find his physician friend and ask him.

The physician of Doc's acquaintance, who lived on the south side of Hyde Park, would pretend to be furious if Doc did not arrive at just the appropriate time between his breakfast and his first patient. Doc did arrive at a good time, however, and as the physician heard him out he discounted the boy's having the plague because, he said, few cases had been reported since the epidemic of 1665. Besides, plague was caused by rats—not that there was any scarcity of rats where the boy was found. Rather, the physician said, it was probably the "fever" (a gen-

eral term applied to unknown maladies of the day)
or consumption, the same was probably true of those
wretches in St. Catherine's, he said. There was just
no way of administering to all the people, the physician
mused, and besides, he was not sure that the masses
should be attended. Perhaps it was intended that their
numbers be kept in check by disease. On the other
hand, as long as people like Doc Bling were willing to
administer to them, then that would more than suffice,
and he himself would not be bothered. His last words
to Doc Bling were chiding remarks about why he
wasted his time worrying about such riffraff. All
the while, however, the physician was measuring out
powders, unguents, linaments, and salves. Doc knew
that the linaments and powders were to be used
sparingly in the sick person's food, and the linaments
also could be rubbed into the chest. He promised to
repay the physician soon with some of his herb tea,
which he often brought the physician to use on his
own patients in very special cases.

Doc had learned over the years to make a syrup of
bark, herbs, and certain roots; when that syrup was
combined with small portions of the healing powder
the fever usually would break within three days, or else
the patient would die. The physician had assured him
many times that such deaths were not caused by the
herbal tea, but that they who died after consuming it
would have died anyway, as would those whom the tea
had made well. The physician used the herbal tea a
great deal himself, but Doc Bling would not divulge

JAMIE IN LONDON • 59

the secret recipe, else there would have been no reciprocation.

As Doc retraced his steps to his own flat, he mused that he must put together the barks, roots, and herbs to brew up another batch of tea, perhaps tomorrow. On his return he found the boy still racked with fever and seemingly unable to move. Throughout the day and early evening he forced a little wheat porridge down the child whenever he could and tried to keep his body cool from the fever but warm from the pervading February cold.

By next morning little change could be noted; so Doc Bling set out to find the ingredients for his tea. He already had bark from a scaly hickory and a wild cherry tree and the roots from a sourdoc plant, but he must find some ratsbane and some mouse-ear. Then there was the secret powdered root he always obtained from the old Chinese man along the river. Before nightfall he had gathered all the ingredients and they were bubbling in the huge pot over the grate. Although the boiling had to be done slowly, and for a very long time, by early evening Doc had skimmed off enough of the tea to try on the boy. He forced some of the liquid down the child; then set out with a flask full for the ill men at St. Katherine's. When he arrived at the depot, however, there was no answer to his knock. He turned away with a heavy heart, assuming that the well men had been shipped out, but he wondered what had happened to those who were ill.

By the following morning the boy could open his

eyes and move his arms and legs about, but he would not try to stand. As Doc busied himself about the flat, he kept up a continuous chatter, asking the lad who he was, where he lived, and what circumstances placed him in the alley behind St. Paul's? The boy never answered, as if he could not speak or did not understand, but his eyes followed Doc around the room. Doc gave the boy more wheat porridge and tea, and on four or five occasions that day he slept; awake, he seemed to grow more calm. By the next morning he sat up, but still did not speak or stand; rather, he just sat and lay there as if bewildered about who the old man was and why he was attending him. On into the evening Doc tried to get the boy to talk, but finally the lad fell asleep still having uttered not a single word.

That night Doc Bling thought long and hard about the situation. He knew that the boy was probably an orphan who had been bought out of the workhouse to be utilized as a chimney sweep or a virtual slave of some other nature, and he could easily see that the boy had been terribly abused, physically. Doc speculated that the boy had run away from his master, living on garbage in the streets until he fell ill and Doc found him in that alley. Harboring such a runaway, however, was a crime for which King George II handed out stiff punishment, and the old man didn't know whether he wanted to risk such a penalty at his age. What did he want with the boy anyway? He would have to furnish him food and clothing, and for what?

Why not turn him over to the authorities? Perhaps he had escaped from just such a depot as St. Katherine's. On the other hand, who, beside his physician friend, knew that the lad was in his flat? Doc was sure that the physician would not divulge any such information. Doc had lent a helping hand to many needy persons before, but none had been in his flat and none had touched his heart as had this lad.

The following morning the boy seemed much stronger. Doc fed him more porridge and tea and then began to speak very firmly to the boy. Doc must know the lad's name, he told him. How old was he? Where did he live? Where had he been? Was he a runaway? When he demanded a name the boy very slowly whispered, "Jamie," but from the tone of voice and the hesitation the old man knew that wasn't his real name. In answer to the question of age the boy shook his head. Did he have a father or mother: Where did he come from? Had he been a chimney sweep? Where was his master? To all such questions Jamie merely shook, his head and indicated great fear, as if preparing to bolt and run, if he could find a way out.

Finally, Doc led Jamie over to the bed and they both sat down. Doc was taken with the boy by now, and he knew it. He told the lad he would be called Jamie, that he could stay with him if he wanted to, and that he need not be afraid anymore. Jamie continued to look very frightened as Doc proceeded to give a brief sketch of his own life to Jamie, describing who he was and what he did. He told Jamie that he could be his apprentice and help gather items for the herbal tea also he could fetch wood and coal for the grate. Jamie smiled then, as Doc went on as if talking to himself. However, Doc knew, and Jamie seemed to understand, that the lad was being given a new identity. He was probably about eight years old, Doc told him, and he probably had no mother or father whom he could remember. He probably grew up in a workhouse or orphanage where he always had been hungry and mistreated. About two or three years before then he probably had been bought out of the place to be used as a chimney sweep, since sores were evident on the knees, elbows, and over most of the body. Through all this Jamie never smiled, but looked bewildered, afraid, and very lonely, with his eyes constantly on the floor. At last, after Doc had kept his arm around Jamie's shoulder for a while, Jamie looked up and moved closer to the old man.

In the days that followed Doc told Jamie to stay in the flat because he didn't want a searching master to find his charge in another man's house. Doc looked for clothes for Jamie in the garbage heaps and alley ways where merchants sometimes lost items of apparel. eventually, however, he gave up and bought Jamie a pair of woolen drawers, two pair of stockings, a pair of shoes, canvas trousers, and a shirt. Due to his shortage of funds, however, all other items of apparel had to be made from what rags they could find.

As February faded into March, the food supply dwindled faster than expected. Also, this late in the winter Doc was having to gather much wood to supplement the meager coal supply. There was enough wheat, their main food item, to last them a while longer, and by spring they would have Jamie well; then they could go together into the country side, where they could buy grain cheaper and perhaps even find some work in the grain fields, where they could breath the good air.

Doc applied salve to Jamie's sores, which soon began to heal. As Jamie grew stronger he kept the flat clean and orderly without having to be told, but he seldom spoke. As usual, Doc kept up a continuous chatter, but Jamie would only smile or look bewildered, as if he didn't understand. Doc could tell that the lad was getting accustomed to a new name, for often he failed to answer to the name Jamie. It was apparent to Doc, watching the boy, that he was learning that there was another world, a world very different from the one he had known until then. Jamie was finding out that he could be loved, even by an old man like Doc, rather than whipped and starved by a hard taskmaster. Close observation told Doc that Jamie didn't understand the words of his continual chatter because the child had no knowledge of this new world, It would be a great challenge to teach him.

Slowly Doc began to agonize about a plan for teaching Jamie about that world which he knew and Jamie didn't. Indeed, he was old, and tired, and lonely, but maybe Jamie was just the audience he needed. Since this might be the greatest challenge he had ever faced as a teacher, he knew he must begin very slowly and be very careful: so he began to plan in his mind: First he would tell Jamie the history of mankind, with a theological explanation for people's being as they were then. Next he would teach him to read and write. Later maybe he would somehow instill in Jamie a desire to learn and investigate for himself. Nevertheless, where and how did one begin with an eight-or nine-year-old child who is totally ignorant of all things but food and fear of a hard taskmaster? How could he make Jamie understand that there was more to life than day-to-day- existence, that each man is his brother's keeper, that the ultimate destiny of man is to rule himself and be free from the dictates of a master, and that the soul is the key to life beyond this earthly life? Was a child of Jamie's nature, background, and obvious simplicity capable of absorbing such high-minded philosophical ideas? Would he want to believe them? Surely this would be a great challenge, and he must begin, but where and how?

As the days passed into weeks, and April arrived, Doc discerned that he had gained a great deal of Jamie's confidence; so he bagan his plan of teaching the boy. First, he told Jamie that, as man's knowledge of himself and the world in which he lived accumulated, each generation passed information on to the next by word of mouth, and later by systematically recording that information, then studying and improving upon the recorded achievements of mankind. He made Jamie understand that he himself was of the latter group, i.e., that he had spent his life studying the recorded history of mankind and trying to determine reasons why people acted as they did.   However, he told Jamie, in order to perform that kind of know-ledge-gathering, his own first task had been learning to read and write.   Thus he made Jamie understand that if he wanted to take advantage of what many great men had learned and recorded before him, first Jamie would have to learn to read and write.

Doc had no children's books—in fact, he had never taught young children—so he began with Chaucer, Plato, Aristotle, and Homer.   Jamie learned quickly, but he much preferred that Doc read aloud to him; then he would ask what certain passages meant. Doc spent many happy hours poring over dozens of books for Jamie's sake, he said, but the fact was that he loved reading for himself alone and was glad for the good excuse to do it.   He read and told Jamie of earliest Civilizations, then that of the spread of coloni-zation and civilization over western Europe, and how the Moslems had intervened from time to time. He told Jamie how people lived in early times and how England was settled by the Angles, the Jutes, and the Saxons.

Intermingled in the history lessons were lessons in theology.   Doc transmitted to Jamie all the history he knew of the Jewish religion, Christianity, and Islam; he especially dwelt on the history of the Roman Catholic Church and its relationship to the known world.   He told Jamie of the Reformation and how, through people's dissatisfaction and unhappiness, Protestant churches such as the Church of England had been founded and had printed their own Bible. He Emphasized the history of England, especially that of the rulers who had broken faith with the Roman Catholic Church and had encouraged many others to withdraw. Doc tried very hard to relate pure history without placing his own interpretation on it, but he found that very hard to do. He told Jamie that he was a Christian insofar as he was not a heathen, Jew, or Moslem, but he was not sure what he believed as to the nature of God and His relationship with man. He was as honest as possible with Jamie when he expressed his belief that surely God existed, but that his understanding of what God was seemed to be unclear. Doc said he believed that people must love and help each other, but whether any one person could interpret God better than another he wasn't quite sure. It was true, of course, that thousands devoted their entire lives to being spokesmen for God and telling others how and why they could best serve God. There wasn't much doubt, he told Jamie, that the Holy Bible was an inspired book, but in his opinion a great part of that inspiration came from King James I's talented translations rather than from God alone. The Bible was a good book which contained wonderful information and thoughts to read and dwell upon, but so did many other books. He even told Jamie that their own closeness, he believed, was the same as being close to God—and maybe that was what life was all about.

He assured Jamie that they would discuss such things often, but ultimately Jamie would have to study them out as he went along life's way, making his own decisions as he was faced with difficult situations.

Each day Doc and Jamie ventured further from the flat, in search of adventure and learning, but also the old man was alert for wood, coal, and other items they could use. Because Doc had no close friends, no one was checking on him, but just in case someone should notice him and the boy, he treated Jamie like an apprentice in public. At home in the flat, however, was another matter, and they both enjoyed the strong bond that was growing between them daily.

By the end of June Doc and Jamie were in the countryside helping with the winter wheat harvest. They bartered labor for grain, and what they could not get by barter they bought with the small amount of money Doc still had. This was Doc's opportunity to give Jamie further lessons about money and English history. He explained how society had changed from the Roman slave system to serfism, then the present system of privately owned and held land, by which, with the sanction of the king, it was hoped that enough food could be grown to sustain the people and the tremendous industrial growth that was taking place in England. He pointed out to Jamie that the peasant class had been—and still were—exploited, probably their exploitation would continue until as a group they had the power to demand a fair price for their labor and the organization to control that power. Doc didn't even hope that Jamie would understand that idea, since he wasn't even sure he did.

As winter approached Doc and Jamie accelerated their storage of food, wood, and coal since they expected to stay indoors a great deal. The London winters were not terribly cold, but they were long and damp, and Doc and Jamie looked forward to a snug closeness approaching. They would read and talk, and go out at least once a day for fresh air. Doc found himself thinking that he was probably more content and fulfilled than he had been in many years, and although he still missed his wife very much after thirteen years, he was growing more fond of Jamie than he had ever thought possible. Jamie learned rapidly and well, and by the spring of 1729 he was beginning to read the classics to Doc.

That summer of 1729 was as nearly a duplicate of the previous one as they could make it. As they worked in the wheat fields and gathered wood, coal, food, and herbs for the winter, they grew fonder of each other daily. They both wanted to scream out their happiness to the world, but there was no one to tell; that in itself made them even closer. Finally, in the fall of that year Doc took Jamie to see the physician. Doc just had to show him to someone; besides Jamie might be required to fetch medicines or deliver his tea. The physician was kind but inquiring of Jamie's background—perhaps too inquiring, Doc thought. He soon dismissed his uneasiness, however, for the physician invited them both to return often and wished them well.

It was that winter of 1729-30 that Doc Bling began to delegate more and more of his work to Jamie. There were days on end that Doc hardly left his straw bed, but he never complained, always reassuring Jamie that he would feel better soon. Although Doc knew the truth, Jamie didn't, and the lad never neglected taking care of Doc. The old man, who was nearing eighty, knew he was nearing his end, but he did so want to live long enough to see Jamie older and more able to care for himself. He knew, however, that he must make preparations for the inevitable; so he concentrated on teaching Jamie everything he could. He taught Jamie about money and had him count the small amount remaining behind the loose brick near the grate. When there was anything to buy, Jamie did it.

As summer came on Doc didn't feel up to going into the countryside, but he was fearful of sending Jamie alone lest he be branded a vagrant or a runaway. Nevertheless they must have food. Finally, Doc decided to write a letter "to whom it may concern", stating that this boy was an apprentice of his physician friend near Hyde Park and that anyone who questioned his identity would be accountable to the physician. Armed with the letter, some money, and precautions from Doc about how to act, the boy went into the countryside alone.

Jamie was questioned a few times concerning his employer, etc, but each time the letter settled the issue. Summer slid into fall while Jamie was busy taking care of Doc and making the usual preparations for winter.

He also learned to make the quarterly rent payments
for the flat. So he and Doc settled in for the winter.
Doc was far from well, however, and he kept growing
weaker. He had no particular ailment; he simply didn't
want to eat. He grew thinner and thinner as Jamie
read to him and fetched for him; he didn't have the
strength to read or even talk much. Jamie made some
tea, with Doc instructing him, but even that didn't
seem to help much. Finally, in early February of 1731
Jamie slipped out early one morning and went to ask
the physician's advice.

The physician listened intently and finally, placing
his hand on the boy's head, he told Jamie to make his
friend Doc Bling as comfortable as he could, for at his
age there was really nothing much more that could be
done medically. Life must end for some and go on for
others. Doc had lived a good life and he should be
granted an honorable and decent death. He told the
lad that he was glad he was with Doc, attending him,
and he wanted to be kept informed about the old man.
Inevitably, one morning in early March 1731, Jamie
arose to find Doc dead on his straw mat. He went to
tell the physician because there was no one else to
tell and nothing else to do.

The physician said he would take care of everything;
then he asked the boy if he would like to stay there
and fetch for him. Jamie only nodded because he had
no notion of what the physician meant or what he would
be expected to do. He was given a small room under
the staircase and instructed to be at the beck and call

of the physician at all times. He was often sent forth into the streets to deliver a paper or medicine; he carried the physician's shield on his person so he would not be taken for a vagrant. Jamie did not tell the physician that for more than a year now he had carried a letter which said he was apprenticed to the physician.

Everything went well for Jamie through the summer, fall, and into the winter, but he missed going to the countryside. Countless times, going about his lonely duties, he repeated to himself the facts and ideas Doc had discussed, fixing them indelibly in his young mind. They would serve him well in years to come, although, at that time they seemed only a poor substitute for reading. He missed the reading, and the books, and Doc, Lord, how he missed Doc. He had no one to talk to, since the physician was always busy; besides, he just didn't have anything to say to the man. He wondered what had happened concerning Doc's burial and the disposal of his books, but was afraid to ask. He had enough to eat, good clothes, and his work was not hard, but he had no close friend. He hadn't told the physician that he still had a few coins of Doc's money either. He wondered many times if he should tell the physician about the money, and ask what had happened to Doc's books, but the wondering never made him reveal that he kept the money tied under his woolen drawers. He sure would like to have those books though.

One morning March 1732 Jamie was making a delivery of medicine to a place near the flat where he and Doc had lived. His curiosity getting the best of him, he went to the flat and peeped in. Maybe the books were still there. He had to lie on the cobblestones to peep into the basement flat, and as he lay there looking at the empty flat and remembering the days and nights he had spent with Doc, he was approached by two men who told him to quickly and quietly get into yonder van (a horse-drawn wagon). He showed them the physician's shield he was wearing and the letter which Doc had written, but they very roughly snatched them from him and placed him in the wagon.

B. A CARGO BOUND FOR THE NEW WORLD

> It is the author's recommendation that, at this point, the reader turn to Appendix A and refresh his/her memory about comparative populations, labor supply and requirements, social conditions in England and western Europe, and English colonialism in America in the early 1700s. Although it is not absolutely necessary to read Appendix A to enjoy this story of Jamie and his travels, it is recommended if the reader is to understand the full import of the migration from Europe to the New World.

It was ironic that Jamie was taken to St. Katherine's and thrown into the very same dungeon that his beloved Doc Bling had visited so many times. Of course, Jamie did not know that; in fact he knew absolutely nothing about what was happening to him. He knew only that he was being detained in a room with about fifty men—some old, some young, some drunk, and many seemingly as scared as he was. No one made it a point to talk to him, and he stayed as far away from the others as he could. Twice each day food was brought into the room, and on a few occasions tobacco and rum were given to selected men.

Well after dark on the third night Jamie was taken with others to a warehouse somewhere along the river, about a thirty-minute walk from St. Katherine's. In preparation for this journey, his hands were tied with a rope which was attached to other men before and behind him. After a few hours in the warehouse, the men were taken aboard a ship. Jamie's experience with ships was limited to the few he had seen in the London port on the River Thames, the little he had read, and what Doc Bling had told him. Therefore, he didn't know the relative size of the ship, whether he was being taken somewhere, or whether he was being brought here to work. He did realize that he was aboard a ship because he recognized the creaking and groaning of timbers, the gentle rise and fall of the floor, and the rocking motion. There was a horrible stench throughout the dungeon-like hold into which he and the others had been placed—even more horrible than that at St. Katherine's. Finally, he realized that, in defiance of governmental authority, in all likelihood he was being shanghaied. Nevertheless, he still huddled to himself as far as possible in the limited space, spoke to no one, and tried, as he had been taught by the hard knocks of life, to be inconspicuous in every way. He simply didn't know what to do or think, but was grateful that up to then the few shillings he had tied in his drawers had not been taken from him.

What Jamie did not know was that an American

colonial plantation owner named Samuel Hope had built his own ship of about two-hundred tons, the *Marywind,* with the notion of transporting tobacco and other American commodities from the Maryland and Virginia colonies to London, then securing from the English crown the right to collect passengers and cargo for the return trip to the colonies. He had plenty of space for transporting paying passengers and cargo (which he preferred), but it was customary for a ship owner to authorize his captain to find persons who could not afford to pay for their passage to America, bind them by contract (permitting themselves to be sold into indentured servitude in return far passage), and use them to fill any remaining space.

As pointed out in Appendix A, many persons were indentured (and legally contracted and bound before a magistrate), and destined for the lowest hold. But if space still remained some captains resorted to kidnapping, spiriting, or shanghaiing persons to fill that space. In most cases the owner didn't know, and some didn't want to know, that such practices were being condoned aboard his ship.

Jamie had been kidnapped and was bound for the American colonies as an unwilling member of an arrangement whereby the ship's captain had forged papers saying that he had been procured legally from a chimney sweep who owned his contract. The forged papers stated that the former master had been paid and that Jamie had willingly submitted to being transported to the American colonies in return for a

reasonable working arrangement and apprenticeship.
Jamie was declared to be eleven, since English law stated that a child between four and fourteen was classified as half-freight. Besides, Mr. Hope would have the
option of selling his services for ten years, since
children were indentured until they were twenty-one.

At that time the formalities of ship departures from
England were simple, whatever cargo they carried. On
its way down the Thames River each ship stopped at
Gravesend, and customs officials (sometimes accompanied by a physician) would come aboard see that
everything was in order. Their duties included inspecting cargo, searching for kidnapped servants, and
ascertaining that all the ship's papers were in order.

Sometimes ships were detained at the Downs for
political reasons; often waiting for special agents who
were not only authorized to question indentured
servants very closely, but was also authorized to free
them. The policy was that each ship waited there (at
the Downs) until reports were taken to London, and
sailing clearance was granted for the ship to continue
down the channel to the open sea. Very often this
wait was long and tedious, sometimes so long as to
cause ships to call at another English port for
supplies before beginning the long ocean voyage.

Jamie remembered Doc Bling's stories of kidnapped servants having told their stories at Gravesend , but none had been believed and released (to
anyone's knowledge), because ship owners always had
sufficiently good stores to convince customs officials

that everything was legal and aboveboard, but the servant had changed his mind and recanted too late. Consequently, when the *Marywind* stopped at Gravesend early in April 1732, Jamie had long since decided not to make a fuss over his being kidnapped, but rather to pretend, as the ship's captain would, that every thing was as it should be. Naturally, the *Marywind's* Papers, including those of properly registered indentured servants, were in order. Therefore, when the paying passengers had been dealt with, and the cargo checked, the customs officials (with tiny pieces of cloth over their noses) came into the hold where Jamie and the fifty or sixty other servants were being transported. When the men asked if anyone had been kidnapped or had any other complaint not a word was uttered by the crowded mass, and clearance was granted to sail.

The *Marywind* stopped at the Downs, as required, and for some reason unknown to Jamie and the others around him, spent two weeks waiting there. Probably Mr. Hope and the ship's captain were the only ones who knew the reason for the delay. The days and nights passed slowly, with Jamie wondering, brooding, and pondering his fate. Still, he kept to himself and spoke to no one.

It was toward the end of April, as best Jamie could figure, when the *Marywind* got under way with quite a hustle and bustle being heard all around. Within two days, however, the ship had stopped again, probably in some English port for more water and food. Jamie and the men in the dungeon-like hold had not yet seen

the light of day since Jamie had entered the dungeon at
St. Katherine's in mid-March. The next day the ship
began to move again, and soon the *Marywind* apparently sailed on the open seas.

The food and water allowance was adequate, and
once every third day Jamie and the others were allowed
a few minutes on the aft deck for fresh air. Seasickness
was everywhere; from what Jamie could detect from his
quarters, and could smell from other parts of the ship,
the greatest causes of the stench were the foul air and
seasickness. The ventilation in Jamie's quarters was
the worst thing to contend with, although all those
around him were terribly miserable from the stench,
fumes, vomiting, fever, seasickness, dysentery, head-
aches, heat, boils, cancer, mouthrot, and the like.
Lice infested every nook and cranny. There was seldom
a night that some of Jamie's neighbors were not carried
out, dead.

By best account that Jamie could command, the
voyage took about twelve weeks; when the ship stopped, approximately the first day of August 1732,
Jamie supposed that they had reached their journey's
end. In actuality the *Marywind* had dropped anchor
in Chesapeake Bay, and preparations were being made
for the ship and the people to enter the harbor at the
mouth of the James River and sail up the river to
Jamestown. Part of the passengers and cargo was
destined for the Virginia colonies in and around James-
town; then the *Marywind* would continue on to Mr.
Hope's plantation in the Maryland colonies further

north. Jamie could hear the feverish activity in the ship overhead, and soon he heard people coming aboard— customs officials, he guessed, like those who had checked the ship when they had departed Gravesend. This activity continued for about two days.

By now Jamie was the only child in his quarters in reasonable physical condition, and there were not more than twenty men who were not sick. However, they were all being fed better and treated better now, and a doctor actually listened to their ailments and administered to them. Quarantine was spoken of—although Jamie didn't know what that meant—but finally the word was passed that it had been decided not to quarantine. Nevertheless, a ship's agent was constantly near, admonishing the servants to eat well and look their best; some were even being coached in their responses when questioned about their trades or handicrafts.

On the third day, the ship began to move again, this time more slowly and apparently on smoother waters. They were proceeding up the James River to unload cargo and dispose of indentured servants. The temperature had become hotter; Jamie could no longer detect any hint of sea breezes, and the heat in the hold was becoming unbearable. In the night the ship stopped again, and come morning Jamie and the twenty or so able-bodied men were taken from their quarters and displayed on the aft deck where they had occasionally gone for air during the voyage. They were made to walk up and down as they were judged as to health, morality, docility, and craftsmanship then the bidding began.

As the day wore on and different bidders came aboard, Jamie could not help noticing that one man, apparently a plantation owner, returned repeatedly and questioned indentured servants very closely. He even asked Jamie his age, which he had been told to say was eleven, and the man asked the ship's agent if there were more servants in the hold, even sick ones. At that, the ship's agent took the bidder away, but within the hour the ship's captain returned with the latter announcing that this man, Sir George Covington, had bought the entire lot, both those on deck and the sick below, for one hundred and twenty-five pounds. Immediately they were unloaded and, while the able-bodied were kept on the docks under watch, the sick were taken away in carts. To breath the fresh air, smell the wonderful aromas, and feel the hot sun seemed like pure heaven to Jamie.

C. INDENTURED SERVITUDE

The details of the transaction of buying the lot of indentured servants were not privileged to Jamie. In fact, he had no concept of the price paid for him versus that which had been paid for the other servants, how long he was to work and where, or even what the word "indentured" implied. Very soon, however, a man in an official-looking uniform, accompanied by Mr. Covington, approached the lot and began to explain conditions of the sale, indenture, and "customs of the country" to the servants huddled on the wharf. He explained that he was an official of His Majesty King George II, a magistrate, and an officer of the Registry of Virginia. He seemed to possess an official document for each of them, and as he talked he made written notes on a separate document as he was talking to each particular man. All these, it seemed, were official records which would be kept somewhere for safekeeping.

In general, each man, as his case came to hand, was told that he was now a bondservant to Mr. Covington for four or five years, that he was to obey Mr. Covington as his master, be a good servant, perform whatever duties he was assigned to the best of his abilities, and be docile and obedient to public law. At the same time he was told that Mr. Covington, as master, was to feed, clothe, and shelter him, be good to him, free him at the end of his indentured contract, and provide him freedom dues according to the customs and laws of Virginia. It was explained to each man that he had the right to air grievances or acts of wrong treatment by his master before any official magistrate of the colony, and Mr. Covington signed the official document in agreement.

Jamie was told that he, being a child of eleven according to his papers and the judgment of the magistrate, was now apprenticed to Mr. Covington for ten years until he was twenty-one, and that he was to work in the tobacco fields where he would have the opportunity to learn how to produce the finest tobacco in all the world. Jamie did not understand what the man was saying during a great part of his explanation; especially he did not understand the meaning of "customs of the country." Therefore, since this subject was an important aspect of indentured servitude, the author will detail an explanation of it at this point, in language as explicit as possible.

Whereas the shackles of ancient caste and privilege gave all rights and privileges to the master and none to the servant, and in that sense were barbarous, the social customs, created solely by Americans, by which the lives of white servants were governed in practically all matters grew gradually with a Christian basis. At first these customs of treatment consisted of a so-called common average, but later they were more carefully and closely defined, often in written indentures but more generally in the domain of magistrates and judges. By 1732 many particulars and specifics had been embodied in acts passed by colonial legislatures and a monument to the peculiar necessities of early Americans had been instituted. Even at James-town, in 1619, the first legislative body in America gave governors instructions that all contracts made in England with respect to white servants, would be duly performed, that violators of contracts would be punished, that provisions of servant's contracts and conditions forbade servants to trade with the Indians, prohibited indentured women (and in some cases men) from marrying without consent of their masters, forbade Sabbath-breaking, and provided for punishment, including whipping, for misdoings. Most of those legislative enactments survived, and by 1624 the laws or "customs of the country" had become very copious. In general, rules were laid down as needed; most frequently they involved fixing the length of time white servants arriving without indentures should remain in bondage and fixing penalties for various crimes, especially running away from a master. There were specific laws dealing with every contingency in careers of indentured servants; they were often referred to as "rights between masters and servants'' as well as ''customs of the country.'' Such codes appeared in Maryland as early as 1638, in Pennsylvania about 1700, in New Jersey about 1714, in New York about 1684, in the Carolinas as early as 1715, and in Georgia about 1796.

For example, the Maryland Assembly in 1638 provided that menservants over eighteen were to serve for four years; if under eighteen, they must serve until they reached age twenty-four. Maid servants over twelve were to serve for four years and those under twelve for seven. Many times ages were required to be judged by a magistrate. At one point, about 1670, five years became the usual term of bondage in Maryland, while some colonies fixed no times but provided that all disputes were to be settled by the local county court. Thus, one can see the variation. For example, if a nineteen-year-old without a contract, came to Virginia in 1700 he served five years, but if he had come to Maryland the same year he would have been required to serve seven years. What is more, there seems to be no rational explanation for these inter-colonial differences, because surely each colony knew of the other's laws. The significant point is that such laws did exist and were enforced.

In short, the status of an indentured servant was that of a chattel of the master, protected both by the terms of his indenture, by the customs of the country, and by the right of appeal or complaint to a county court or to a migistrate of any locality. Except in special cases in Pennsylvania and New York, his service could be bought and sold freely, he could be used to pay off a debt, or a sheriff could take him to satisfy a master's debt. He could not vote, hold office, or serve on juries. Because he could be disposed of at will, he was often the stake at a card game. Generally, he could hold property but could not engage in trade, since presumably he could embezzle his master's goods. Spare-time money earned by any servant was often subject to confiscation by a master, and runaways suffered severe penalties. The servant was often subject to serve in the militia, and he was liable to the public, as well as to the master, for public crimes. Virginia, especially, prohibited the private burial of dead servants, lest the master conceal evidences of murderous treatments; statutes of some colonies even provided that a maimed or disfigured servant must be set free. The amount of food and clothing to be provided was regulated very strictly in some places, but generally was left to customs of the country.

One important custom of the country concerned fixing the amount of freedom dues given servants at the expiration of their terms. Most indentures specified such dues to be according to the customs of that particular plantation. Smith, in his research, found such widespread differences in practice and considered them of such importance that he assembled the information in tabular form Appendix C. The peculiarity here is that land grants were mentioned in some statutes and not in others, supposedly because few colonies had the power to grant land. This fact may account for the absence of such provisions for freed servants in Virginia during the seventeenth century, but in general it was the intention of all colonies to equip the freed servant with the ability to earn wages sufficient to buy a plot of land very soon after being freed.

Thus, we see the general outline of the servant's status in the colonies, his expectations according to the customs of the country, and especially his recourse to the laws of the land. The real question, however, concerned the effectivness of these regulations; that is, was a servant really protected from cruelty and exploitation, and did his right to complain to any local magistrate mean that he really could go to a magistrate and be given justice: Few generalizations can be made about these points, but Smith ventured his opinion that, by and large, when servants had indentures in proper form, the provisions were upheld and enforced by courts. Customs of the country protected those without indentures, and fear of a master did not seem to deter servants from consulting magistrates or other officials. The most prevalent complaints, both by servants with proper indentures and by those without them, concerned freedom dues, and generally the court upheld the servant. As mentioned previously, servants were not afraid to go to the magistrates with their complaints, and the fact that a large proportion of servants won their cases in court is a credit to the system, for it must be understood that the servant was almost always appearing against a member of the magistrate's own class (most likely one of his friends or neighbors). Also, it must be understood that we are speaking of the strictly legal aspects of the servant's existence and whether or not he received fair treatment before the court. This does not mean that there were no troubles, no exploitation, no mistreatment but merely refutes the often prevalent argument that servants were largely unprotected from the arbitrary and capricious tyrannies of their master.

No person knowledgeable of the history of that time would deny that indentured servants suffered many more cruelties and hardships than they should have suffered, many of which were not redressed by constituted authority. There is ample evidence that the examples of fair treatment can be matched by as many examples of great misery. Suffice it to say, therefore, that one can find in the records an example of almost anything for which he looks, in this respect. For example, some writers state that Maryland court records show that a great number of indentured servants committed suicide, whereas, in Jamie's time, John Hammond announced that none had gone to the Virginia colony without recommending the place in letters to their friends, and urging them to come.

It must be remembered, also, that of all the things which caused misery to white servants, the first and most important was neither the temper of their masters nor the unfairness of magistrates but simply the climate of the country. In England, men and women of menial status were accustomed to obeying masters and often suffering grevious cruelties from them, but they were not acclimated to the heat and glare of the subtropical summer temperatures of Virginia. Mortality from fevers and pestilence was high; eventually experience taught that the best time to land servants was the beginning of the winter season. However, Jamie's group was landed in August, probably the hottest month of the entire year.

Jamie and the others slept in a warehouse near the wharf that night, and the following morning they were taken to the Covington plantation, which he soon learned was called "the Savedge" because, located on the edge of the swamps and woodlands of Surry (later to become Surry County, Virginia), it was then being carved out of that wilderness.

The trip to the Savedge took most of the day; Jamie and the men walked two abreast along a wagon trail, with a two-wheeled cart in front and one bringing up the rear. The servants were allowed to stop and rest about ten minutes out of each hour. Toward the day's end, as a few cumulus clouds partially screened the blistering sun, the new servants topped a rise and saw the plantation, their plantation, the Savedge, spread out below them, covering the whole valley and reaching to the river beyond. Patches of trees here and there hid the edges of fields partially, but the plantation covered more ground than Jamie could see. Two of the nineteen men who had started with him that morn-

ing had fallen out during the trek and been picked up
by the rear cart. Now the servants saw their new home
for the first time. They had stopped to rest again, and
Jamie took this opportunity to try to orient himself.
The men driving the carts (Jamie didn't know whether
they were servants or freemen) explained nothing.
Jamie assumed correctly that the huge house on a
small knoll near the river was Mr. Covington's manor-
house; smaller houses could be seen between the man-
sion and the warehouse along the river.

The new servants were taken to one of the cabins
and were instructed to take off their shirts and wash
up. When they had done this they were given fresh,
clean shirts, and women had set food before them on
the long tables standing in front of each cabin. The
food was a loblolly of ground corn mush; there was a
sweet juice, which Jamie would later know was cane,
to drink. Soon, two men came to bring each servant a
blanket and tell them all that they were to sleep in the
cabin in front of which they had eaten. The building
was long and narrow with a row of rough, wooden
bunks down each side. Each bunk had a straw mat
on it.

The entire situation was strange in that ever since
leaving England none of the servants had made friends
with any other, and there was very little talk. Even
now, as each chose a sleeping place in the cabin, there
was virtual silence except for the men muttering to
themselves. It was as if no one knew what to do,
or say, or expect; for the first time in their lives no one

was standing over them telling them every move to make. There was no need asking each other what to expect, because it seemed understood that no one knew; so they all lay on their bunks and were soon asleep.

Jamie was awakened at 5:00 A.M. by the ringing of a bell and someone saying that breakfast was coming. He soon learned that such was the custom except for Sunday morning, when the bell rang for church at 9:00 A.M. Although Jamie did not know it then, Saturday afternoons and Sundays were free from labor in all the colonies. Breakfast consisted of the same loblolly, with a few bits of pork, thrown in. After they ate, they lounged there at the table or wandered back into the cabin. Soon, however, a second bell rang, and the word was passed that each servant was to line up in front of the table. Jamie soon learned that this was the work bell which rang at 6:00 A.M. to signal the beginning of the workday. He could see a similar group of men, with a sprinkling of women among them, near each cabin. A man approached and told them that he was John, chief overseer for Mr. Covington. John picked fifteen men whom he said he was taking for work detail; that left only two sickly looking men and Jamie. The two sick ones were told to go to the cabin where a red banner was flying in the breeze and ask for medicine and instructions. Jamie was told to wait for the tobacco crew. In a few minutes, however, a woman came and instructed him to go the the tobacco field yonder and ask for Timothy.

Everything about him was a wonder to Jamie: The soil, with its texture and warmth; the trees; the foliage; the vines along the seeping streams or marshes; the crops of all kinds, of which Jamie knew little, reaching as far as he could see; and the sun, already burning, scorching, and blistering without mercy. All this flooded his mind. He wore the trousers and shoes which had been given him before leaving England the shirt of the night before, and he still had Doc Bling's few shillings tied in his crotch beneath his underwear, but he had nothing to shield his head from the scorching rays of the sun. He did as he had been told, however, and walked briskly to the tobacco field, where about twenty men were going about their work. Approaching the obvious overseer, he announced that he was Jamie, instructed to seek Timothy. As the overseer turned and agreed that he was indeed Timothy, and that he had already been told about Jamie, he looked the lad over carefully. "I've been told to make a tobacco man outta ya, and that'll take some doing, I expect. Don't you have a hat, boy—Jamie?" All the while he was fashioning a hat for Jamie from a tobacco leaf.

Jamie soon learned that Timothy, himself a freed servant, was a kind man completely in charge of all the tobacco grown on the Savedge. He was known to chastise the servants, but seldom, if ever, unjustly. Some overseers of that time would beat a servant about the head with a cane til the blood flowed, for a fault not worth the speaking of; yet the victim must have patience or worse might follow.

Timothy explained to Jamie that they were presently suckering the tobacco, getting ready to top it the next week, and that they would cut it in about a month. He told Jamie to work steadily but not too rapidly, lest he get sunstroke, watch what the others were doing and imitate them, and by all means ask questions. However, as if it were an afterthought, he said, "Maybe if I wuz you I'd be about a week before I started asking, then you'd be more likely to know what to ask."

Jamie broke the suckers and threw them on the ground as the others were doing, and soon the older and bigger men were prevailing upon him to sit and crawl and pluck the suckers nearest the ground, thereby saving them from bending. They rested a few minutes each hour; then just before 11:00 A.M. Timothy rang the bell and told them to rest for about three hours through the heat of the day. Jamie now went with the tobacco crew rather than back to his first cabin. A maidservant served them the same loblolly and carried away the utensils when they had finished. Jamie rested and wondered. He wondered about himself and if he could really please Timothy and the others in the tobacco fields; he wondered what would eventually happen to him; most of all he wonderred if that eternal hot sun would ever cease shining.

On returning to work after midday, Timothy brought Jamie a cap. As they entered the tobacco fields, the overseer told the other servants that Jamie, being apprenticed to learn the tobacco business from him, would henceforth fetch and carry for himself alone. He said that when Jamie was not otherwise busy he could help them with a difficult chore, but for the most part his job would be to help the overseer. This pleased Jamie very much, but all the same, he still pulled suckers when he was not fetching for timothy. At nearly 7:00 P.M.the bell rang again, this time for quitting and going to the cabin for supper.

As the days passed Jamie hid the few shillings which Doc Bling had left him, changing the hiding place often, and he worked ceaselessly. He kept near Timothy, mostly in fear that the other servants might attempt to harm him. He watched many strong looking men grow weak and sick with the fever, and eventually be taken to the cabin with the red banner. When he himself had a touch of the fever for two or three days Timothy took him for doctoring and made him rest in the cabin. He recuperated quickly, however, and was soon back at Timothy's heels. Within the first few months both boy and man could feel the growing attachment between them. Jamie began to be bold enough to ask questions here and there, and Timothy seemed all too pleased to be able to teach this bright young lad the ways of the New World, and of this plantation and its tobacco in particular.

Timothy told him that he was a Scotsman who had come to Virginia as an indentured servant almost twenty years before, but had been a freeman then for more than fourteen years. He could plainly see that

Jamie was a bright young man, and he admonished him to keep a sharp eye out and observe all things around him. Actually, he saw that such practices seemingly had been inbred in Jamie and knew that he was only encouraging them. In a fashion, Timothy took up where Doc Bling had left off almost two years before, and took Jamie under his wing. Whereas Doc Bling had been a man of thought and letters, Timothy was a man of brawn and action. He provided another side of life for Jamie.

Timothy pointed out that the great requirement for servants on all the colonial plantations was to work in the fields; it was common knowledge and good sense that a good man who could chop logs was more valuable than an artisan or clerk. Also, he pointed out that women servants had slightly less burdens to bear than men because they were not worked in the field unless they were nasty, beastly, and not fit for other services. Timothy said he wanted no woman in his tobacco field because there were certain things they just could not learn to do. For example, he explained, next winter Jamie would learn to chop, fell trees, clear land of brush, and turn new soil, but a woman simply could not perform those chores well. He also pointed out that he himself had been a man of the earth all his life, and that the hours of labor, advantages, and other conditions for agricultural workers were much better here than in Europe. Besides, he reminded Jamie, the Savedge tobacco was known all over the world as the best. He believed that was mostly due to the fact that only men with a true love for tobacco were used in its cultivation.

Another tenet of his philosophy which Timothy revealed gradually over the months was that there were, in general, three kinds of servants. There were those who had been bred to the land; they found this new life enjoyable. There were those who had been trained as artisans and later forced to become field hands; only about half of those endured and survived. Finally, there were those who had been theives, pick pockets, vagrants, and rogues; little sympathy should be wasted on them because they seldom endured the terms of their indenture, and if they did, they usually returned to their old ways, either in the colonies or back in Europe. It was Timothy's hope that Jamie would take to the land, be a good servant, and thereby learn to be a good tobacco man. There was every possibility, the overseer assured him, that some day he could own his own land and grow his own tobacco. Timothy himself owned some land and was using his wages as overseer for Mr. Covington to pay for it. An arrangement had been worked out whereby he was renting that land to Mr. Covington until it was paid for and he could afford to work for himself.

During those fall months of 1732, Timothy patiently explained to Jamie how tobacco was grown, cared for, and readied for barter, sale, or shipment. At this time tobacco was just coming into its own in the world market; therefore Jamie had been plunged unknowingly into the abyss of tobacco history. Timothy

pointed out that many of the largest and prettiest tobacco plants, now standing head-high to a man and in
full bloom would be allowed to stand and go to seed.
Later, about October, those seed would be gathered
carefully and saved to sow in a bed the next February.
As the seed germinated and grew the next plants
would be protected from the frost, which would occur
until about mid-April. In the meantime, the tobacco
fields would be prepared, with rows laid out to receive
the plants, which would be plucked from the seed bed
and transplanted to the fields in May. Then the tobacco
plants would be cultivated, plowed, hoed, wormed,
suckered, and generally cared for daily until they
reached their present point of full bloom.

Next week the workers would break the top from
each plant except those to be saved for seed and continue to pull suckers, which grew where each leaf
emerged from the stalk itself. By mid-September the
crop would begin to ripen, as evidenced by the leaves
thickening and turning yellow, beginning with the
bottom most leaves and progressing up the stalk.
As they ripened, the leaves would be plucked, carefully laid out, and hauled by man-pulled carts, to the
tobacco barns where they would be strung up on rope
or wire to dry. By the end of September each stalk
would have been stripped of about half its leaves;
then the entire stalk would be cut and taken to the
barns for the remainder of the leaves to dry while
still attached to the stalk. By November or early
December the tobacco leaves would be sufficiently

cured to be tied into "hand," or bundles, but only when they were at the right dampness not to crumble; then the hands would be stacked neatly, graded according to likeness of quality. At this point the tobacco was placed in crates in the warehouses along the river where Mr. Covington would sell it, keep it, trade it, use it to pay debts, or sometimes store it for a better market. Timothy's tobacco was the best in Virginia, Mr. Covington bragged.

The fall passed rapidly for Jamie, who as a bright young lad nearing fourteen flourished under Timothy's guidance. The other servants working in the tobacco fields and barns mostly ignored Jamie because they knew by then that Timothy would tolerate no interference in the teaching of his protégé.

Through the fall and early winter they labored with the tobacco as usual, but in January Timothy announced that the tobacco field used the year before was worn out (usually tobacco was grown on new land for three or four years; then the land was turned over to sugar cane production) and they would clear a new field of six or seven acres for the coming year's crop. Of course this preparation of new land for planting was unfamiliar to Jamie, who engaged in every phase with much zeal. Trees had to be felled, trimmed, and dragged away; brush had to be cleared and burned; most of this work was accomplished by man's muscle, since there were few animals for such chores. It was then that Jamie learned to use an axe, and Timothy bragged that the lad learned to "chop like a man" in the short-

est time he had ever seen. When all the clearing
and burning was done, the ground was then turned,
mostly with makeshift plows and man's muscle power.
Timothy explained to Jamie that the skilled American
axman and preparer of new soil was a colonial product,
not a European importation, since the art of clearing,
plowing, and preparing the soil had been learned
largely from the Indians.

The new land was strong and fertile, with hundreds
of large waist-high stumps. The great problem was
that wild extraneous bushes and weeds would grow
naturally, choking out the young tobacco plants, unless
continually chopped out. That chopping was the culti-
vating chore which occupied most of the summer.

Thus Jamie labored and grew stronger and wiser
under timothy's tutelage. On occasion he would be
loaned to the cane fields or mills, or the cornfields,
or sometimes he would help mix mortar for building
a fence or foundation, but he was always glad when he
could return to the tobacco crew and Timothy. He
began to make friends with the other servants, one a
German countryman, one a former man of letters
much like Doc Bling, and one the Scotsman Tob,
much like Timothy, who also was nearing the end of
his indenture. He had very little contact with women,
however, seeing them only at mess time or at some
distance on the Sabbath, when everyone was required
to attend church services, which often were held under
a tree somewhere on the Savedge.

From time to time Jamie would hear of servants

being punished for misdoings, or running away and being caught and whipped; many times he saw strong men faint at their labors. On at least one occasion he heard that servants on a nearby plantation, having mounted a concerted rebellion against mistreatment and over work, had tried to kill their master, but the rebellion had not succeeded. Such an idea was foreign to Jamie, because his working conditions and treatment were good. He had meat three times a week, and he had reasonably good clothes to wear. He saw servants freed to collect their freedom dues in tobacco or sugar, the customary dues on the Savedge, and he saw or heard of many servants being sent to the militia. The word among the servants was that one could disobey, shirk assigned duties, or break fairly stringent laws, and in each case receive reasonable punishment; for a runaway servant who was caught, however, almost any penalty could be inflicted. Probably for this reason there were comparatively few runaways.

So the years passed as Jamie labored at his assigned duties as a bond servant on the Savedge. When he was about seventeen Timothy left the Savedge to work his own land, and a new overseer came to manage the tobacco fields. The new man was much like Timothy although somewhat more prone to temper-quick punishments. Jamie, however, being the bright young man that he was, did his job well and gave no cause for undue punishment. Because the new overseer respected Jamie's brawn, good nature, and ability to read and write, they learned from each other.

Jamie often reflected that he discovered something new every day from the people and the country around him. At the same time, he had never allowed himself to forget the lessons in history, geography, theology, and philosophy which his old friend Doc Bling had impressed upon his childish mind years before.

At twenty, still working the Savedge tobacco fields, he was known as one of the best servants on the plantation—good with an axe and with every aspect of growing and caring for good tobacco.

D. JAMIE'S FLIGHT WESTWARD

Jamie was about twenty, six foot tall, weighed 170, and could work and lift circles around any man, when he admitted, in the spring of 1740, a longing to be free. He dreamed of a different sort of freedom than he expected in another year. For more than eight years he had kept the few shillings of Doc Bling's hidden— and in the past two years he had squirreled away tobacco and cane seed, dried meat, and a pouch of "nocake."* He had read everything available, including a King James Version of the Bible loaned to him occasionally, and he had thought and rethought of Doc

*Early colonial writers and travelers told of a particular way of using corn which showed how necessary it was and how much people depended on it. To prepare it, Indian corn was parched in hot ashes, beaten into a powder and poured into a long leather bag trussed at a man's back like a knapsack. It was the most nourishing food known, in the most compact form, for three spoonfuls a day mixed with snow in winter and water in summer, adequately fed both Indians and white men on long journeys. Samp, a meal pottage made from unparched corn, could not be dried and preserved for long storage as was nocake.

Bling's lessons a thousand time over. Night after night he seemed to hear Doc Bling telling him again that man was born to be free, to be his own master, and to live by the fruits of his own planning and labor. After Timothy's departure he had been even more lonely and restless, and these thoughts had become so important that finally he knew he could wait no longer for the freedom he craved. So it was, in early May, that he left the Savedge, walking away into the moonless night with an axe, a knapsack containing his few shillings, some tobacco seed and cane seed, the tattered remains of a Bible, some dried meat, and a pouch of nocake.

If someone had asked Jamie why he was embarking upon that risky venture, he probably would have replied that he was driven by some great compelling forces which he could not explain. Later analysis of his actions revealed what he didn't understand at that time: the compelling forces were, first, a need for intimate companionship—someone to talk to, love, and share his innermost secrets— and second, the feeling of accomplishment generated by proving that, with no one telling him what to do, he could live by his own wits and govern himself as his own master. All he knew in fact, that May night, was that there was a void in his life, and he must begin searching for whatever would fill that void.

He knew that he would have to travel westward into unknown and uncharted territory, avoid all people, live by his own wits, and never look back. Aware that he was totally ignorant both of the country into which he was fleeing and of the ways of the Indians who inhabited it, he found himself not only willing to take the risk, welcoming it as a challenge to be met and conquered. His knowledge of plantation life, and especially the culture of tobacco, was vast, but of the great expanse toward which he now looked, his knowledge and plans were weak and vague indeed. He had seen Indians on rare occasions, and he had heard many stories both of Indians who had treated the white man well and of Indians who had killed or held in slavery every white man who had ventured into their territory. He had heard stories of runaway servants being sent back to their masters for ransom, but of course he was not priviledged to know whether any runaway servants had ever lived in harmony with the Indians as they made lives of their own in the wilderness. Of the wilderness itself, he had heard stories of great mountains and wide rivers which even the Indians could not conquer.

As he struck out over the hills of southeastern Virginia the night was beautiful; the starlight showed the leaves on the trees were about half-grown, and everything was pretty and alive. The spring rains had just ended, and every plant and tree seemed strained to bursting with summer growth. The night reminded Jamie that he had often thought it would be like this to go on a pleasure stroll around the plantation, with no one to bother or hinder him. Nevertheless, he was on his guard every minute for unusual sights and sounds, although what might be unusual Jamie had not the slightest idea. Actually as he absorbed the sounds of the animals and the dimly seen sights of the magnificent forest and rolling hills around him, he was listening for human sounds but heard none save his own.

That first night under the stars he slept in a hollow tree which had been blown off by lightening about ten feet above the ground. He got cold and didn't sleep much, actually, but by daybreak he was rested and eager to resume his venture. He had no trouble snaring a rabbit for breakfast, for they were so plentiful that they almost came up and ate from his hand. He had more trouble making a fire from flint and moss, but he finally feasted on rabbit.

He knew that already he would have been missed at the plantation, that a search had been mounted for him, and that runaway posters would soon appear, but with less than a year of indenture still owing to Mr. Covington, he knew that the search would be limited to Virginia and, perhaps, Maryland. He knew also that very likely no one would think that he had fled into the wilderness; even if the idea should occur to anyone, going after him probably would not be worth the bother. Therefore, Jamie knew that his greatest danger lay in being captured by the Indians, who would kill him, make him their slave, or trade him to white officials for return to Mr. Covington. He would have to be very careful, he knew, for being returned to Mr. Covington would cause him to be whipped and probably would extend his indenture—perhaps as much as seven more years—and certainly he didn't want that. On the other hand, neither did he want to be killed or enslaved by the red man. He knew that he had a lot of learning to do, but if God went with him, he would make it.

Oh, yes, Jamie had come to believe that there was a God who watched over and provided for all mankind, and that man in turn had a debt to God for the bounty He had placed on earth for use. He had pieced together his own philosophy from things Doc Bling had told him long ago, from mandatory church attendance on the plantation, and from reading the tattered King James Version of the Holy Bible which was made available to him on rare occasions. He believed, as Doc Bling had taught him long ago, that man was responsible only to God for his actions; that no man should be subject to another man's will, but only to God's; that man was born to live in harmony with other men, and in that sense was his brother's keeper; and that the soul was the key to life beyond the grave. He wasn't exactly sure, though, what he believed about life eternal. He had worried about that a great deal and had never been able to come to an absolute conclusion, but right now he had trouble enough with this life, without having to think about a life hereafter.

For five days Jamie traveled westward, bearing slightly left of the point where the sun went down, as rapidly as caution would allow. By then he figured he was a hundred miles or more from the Savedge and could slow down slightly. In that time he had crossed dozens of small creeks and narrow rivers, had waded swamps for hours at a time, and on two occasions had heard the unmistakable sounds of civilization nearby. In both instances he quickly doubled back, avoiding all contact with or sight of humankind. On the fourth day he had experienced some difficulty half wading and half swimming across a rather large river. That night he was certain that he was near an Indian camp, for he could smell smoke and hear an occasional sound not of the forest and animals. Worried, he made no fire, ate only from his nocake, rested under a ledge of outcropping of rocks, and slept very little. By daybreak he was quietly on his way again.

The fifth day was uneventful, except for negotiating the ever-present creeks and swamps, listening to the animals, admiring the giant trees, and relishing the realization that to a certain extent he could slow down and relax. He was now coming into more hilly country, and he began to find it necessary to follow streams for his trail, and occasionally to climb and cross ridges seeking another valley lying more nearly in the direction he wanted to go. He oriented himself on the setting sun each day and aimed just to the south or left of that line. On the eleventh day, having crossed six creeks, near sundown he came to the foot of a rather high summit, which he climbed in order to spend the night there, orient himself regarding the nature of the countryside nearby, and plan his further route. The setting sun was never more beautiful as it lighted up a high mountain far to the southwest. Even though that mountain was south of his planned course, Jamie decided to aim for the top of that mountain and there orient himself again.

Four hard days travel later he reached the top of the mountain, where the elevation made him somewhat light-headed and caused difficulty in breathing. Nevertheless, from a huge jutting rock he discovered a magnificent western view; a single high mountain rose to the northwest, and directly west a succession of small ridges gradually grew into higher mountains; still further west, a massive mountain range loomed in the blue haze. Maybe this was the great mountain range of which he had heard where, the stories proclaimed, the rivers parted and flowed in different directions, where Indians commanded the mountains and all the land west thereof—an unknown boundary of land where few, if any, white men had ever trod. Needless to say, those tales were stored in Jamie's mind as great treasures, and he wanted to see those mountains and that great land beyond.

Provided the stories he had heard were in any way true, if he headed west into the foothills and toward the great mountains, it would be to his advantage to find a large river and travel upstream, for it would be flowing eastward down out of the mountains. On the fourth day thereafter he discovered what he believed to be such a stream, but soon thereafter he found it leading him in circles. Finally, in desperation, he left the stream and struck out north over some of the low mountain ranges hoping to discover a large river leading into the mountains. Jamie knew that, having virtually lost his original direction, he was wandering aimlessly now, and he was beginning to grow more weary; he wanted to stop to rest somewhere for an extended period of time. It must be early in June now; on the Savedge they would be setting the tobacco and getting ready, in general, for the hot summer ahead. Here in the mountains, however, it was cool—sometimes much colder than Jamie liked at night.

Actually, in the far reaches of his mind Jamie came to realize that he was beginning to search for a place to spend the summer and prepare for the coming winter, for surely, as cool as the weather was in June, it would be much colder in the mountains this winter than it was on the Savedge. He knew that he would have to gather, prepare, and store up a certain amount of food by drying fruit and berries, and laying away roots and tubers. He was progressing fewer and fewer miles each day now, and the great mountain range still loomed before him as a tremendous obstacle. His plans were changing though, and he found himself thinking about finding a refuge—a base from which he could explore until he tackled the mountain the next spring. In his wanderings he came upon a new river and this time he followed it downstream, only to find that it was flowing north. For about a week he followed this river north before reaching its confluence with a major branch of the stream. When he decided to proceed up the newly found tributary he found that he was again headed southwest, the direction he had preferred from the very beginning.

On his third day of traveling up the tributary Jamie began to find evidence of old campsites and footprints leading into the river. He inspected these from under the cover of brush and trees and from as great a distance as possible. Without doubt, these were signs either that Indians were nearby or had been living here recently. Some footprints were made by bare feet; still others seemed to have been made by a flat-soled, soft shoe with no heel. He crept forward very cautiously now. Dozens of times he thought of turning back or changing directions, but then he decided that this was a trial he would have to meet and overcome; so he crept along the hillside about two hundred yards from the river, where the forest was more open and he could keep an eye all about him. His only weapons were his short-handled axe and the stick he carried to help him walk and climb.

Jamie was being very careful, he thought, creeping from one large tree to another, constantly watching the river. Suddenly, without warning, something tore into his right shoulder, followed immediately by something tearing into his left foot. Both projectiles had struck glancing blows from the rear, doing painfully harmful damage but not having lodged in the flesh; so Jamie had no choice but to strike out forward, running fast as he could. He never looked back, but soon he could hear sounds of being chased, of men breaking through the forest and of voices yelling unintelligible words. The excruciating pain in his foot was greatly hampering his running, and his shoulder began aching as a numbness crept down his right arm.

On he went, blindly tearing through the underbrush as fast as he could. He thought that he was bearing away from the river, but he had no plan except trying to outdistance his pursuers. After what seemed about an hour, however, he was near exhaustion when suddenly he found himself going straight into the river. That was not part of his plan, but he could not stop now; so he eased into the water and crept down the river, holding to reeds and overhanging bushes along the edge. It was not long before his pursuers reached the riverbank where Jamie had entered, and he could hear them chattering excitedly. Judging from the sound, there must have been more than a dozen men; Jamie sensed that they were trying to guess whether he had gone across, up, or down the river. They weren't more than a hundred yards away when Jamie, who kept edging down stream, heard them apparently agree to split up, with half going up the river and half going down.

As Jamie eased further down the river he found that he was entering a very deep narrow, almost lake-like area; just over his head a very high bank extended far back into the woods. Quickly he figured out that his pursuers would have to detour quite a distance into the woods to bypass that high bank before coming to the river again at a point some distance below this location. Therefore, he decided that his only choice was to strike out across the river, swimming underwater as much as possible in hope of reaching the opposite bank without being detected. He reached the opposite bank and pulled himself up under an overhanging tree just as the Indian party reached the riverbank some distance below where Jamie had departed a few minutes before.

Jamie could see the six or eight men armed with bows and hatchets as they waded into the river to peer up and down. Further up the river he could hear the other party searching and muttering, but they were not in sight. Long minutes passed as Jamie, in great pain, huddled under the overhanging tree; finally the men decided to proceed downriver. Soon they were out of sight and almost out of hearing, and Jamie had begun to think about climbing the riverbank and inspecting his wounds, when the party that had gone upriver appeared again; so Jamie remained in the water for about an hour before all the Indians had gone down the far riverbank, out of sight and hearing.

When Jamie had pulled himself up the high bank and had found a fallen tree to lie behind, he inspected his wounds. Taking off his knapsack with his left hand because his right arm, in terrible pain, was completely useless, he determined. Upon examination of his left foot, he found that part of his shoe had been torn away and some of the tendons of his heel apparently had been severed. He knew that if he stayed there he would be found by the Indians, and if he moved, either he would leave a trail of blood which surely would cause him to be found, or he would die of exhaustion. His first objective, therefore, became exercise, both to get warm (for he was suddenly deathly chilly because of loss of blood) and at the same time to search for a better hiding place. So he dragged himself up the mountainside, inch by inch, for what seemed an eternity.

The pain was still there, but he was no longer chilling. Even though he was in a dense forest, he could tell that the sun was setting, and he knew that he must find a place to spend the night before he collapsed from pain and exhaustion. Still pulling himself up the mountain and away from the river, Jamie came to a huge overhanging rock, almost like the projecting roof of a house. As he hauled himself under the enormous rock, he found that he was in the mouth of a cave; now everything seemed strangely quiet and peaceful, and he was warm again. He felt a strong demand to sleep, if even for only a few minutes; then he would arouse and prepare himself for the night.

Jamie woke with a start—and the feeling that he was not alone. There was a peculiar inky darkness all around him, and glowing embers of a fire were almost within his reach. He lay on some kind of animal skin and another skin covered him. Since darkness around him was not that of night in the forest, Jamie quickly surmised that he must be in a cave. However, he couldn't remember building a fire, and certainly he didn't own an animal skin for a bed. The last thing he remembered was the terrible pain in his shoulder and foot, along with the weariness. He flexed his right arm and found that it had feeling and that his shoulder, though stiff, did not hurt. He moved his left foot to find it sore but not hurting. His mind raced to figure out where he was, what was happening, and what to do. He was raised on his elbows staring into the inky darkness when a sound drew his attention to the vicinity of the bed of coals.

Jamie could see a human form standing just beyond the fire, and as the form slowly approached, he could tell that it was that of a woman. As she stood in the dying light it was apparent that she was a white woman dressed in Indian clothing. Her age was a puzzle to Jamie, but with her black hair pulled tightly back from her face and tied in back and her arms folded, each up the opposite sleeve, she appeared ageless. In a quiet, halting voice—speaking in good English—she told Jamie that he should not be afraid of her, that he must think of her as his friend, that he must not move because of his wounds, and that she would return soon with food and water; then she disappeared into the darkness.

In the hours immediately following, Jamie's mind raced as it never had before. Who was this woman? Was she really a friend, or would she betray him to the Indians? How long had he been here? Should he strike out again and flee further into the mountains, or was the woman right about his wounds not being sufficiently healed? He tried to stand, but found that he was too dizzy and that his shoulder and foot did indeed hurt very badly, except when he was lying down. It wasn't long, therefore, before Jamie knew that he had no choice but to believe in the woman and beg of time to let his wounds heal.

Jamie didn't know how many hours later he woke, just as before, to find the woman in the shadows. She came to his side and offered him samp—a type of corn mush—and water. Jamie found that he was very hungry, and as he ate, propped on one elbow, the woman began to talk, very slowly and softly. Although she spoke good English, she seemed so unaccustomed to using the words that she seemed to search for each one.

The woman told Jamie that she had discovered his trail out of the river and found him, delirious with fever, by the cave entrance five days before. She had dragged him further into the cave and since then had tended him at least once each day, forcing him to eat and drink, even if but a little each time. He was now past the fever, she said, but it would be some time before his wounds would be healed enough to travel. She would bring him food and water until he could provide for himself, but he must not plan on traveling any distance for a month or more. She must go now, she said, and she would come again as soon as she could. Before Jamie could speak she again faded into the darkness of the cave just as quickly and mysteriously as she had appeared.

Jamie ate some samp and drank the water she had left him. Feeling much better, he exercised his arms and legs without trying to stand. He realized he was much stronger, but also he was sleepy. When he awoke again it was with the same feeling that the woman was present, and sure enough, as he rose on his elbow, he saw her in the shadows. Coming forward slowly, this time she smiled as she handed him more food and water. Very quickly, Jamie opened the conversation by asking who she was.

The woman said that she was a Christian white woman named Mary, born in Scotland of vey poor parents about 1700. She was sold into servitude when she was about sixteen and brought to Albermarle (now North Carolina), where she served a harsh master for six years, bearing him three children during that time. For the past eighteen years she had been with the Cherokee Indians, having been traded in 1722 as a wife for the chieftain's son.

She had borne three sons to her Indian husband, but none of them lived now. The smallpox epidemic of 1738 had taken the last of them. She lived now about a mile up the river in a Cherokee village where her husband had become chief. Although her status had always been that of second wife, she still was a respected member of the tribe. In her tribe there was a sixteen-year-old girl called Little Deer, who was referred to as "Mary's child." That was not really true, she said. She had suckled the child and raised her from a few-months-old baby, but she didn't know where Little Deer had come from; no doubt she had been stolen or taken as hostage when they had killed her mother in a raid. Anyway, when she was seventeen, Little Deer was to become the wife of one of the Indian braves at the fall harvest festival, or Green Corn Ceremony. Mary confessed that she had tried to escape the Cherokees many years ago, but they had found her and as punishment had cut off all the toes on her right foot. Now she was growing old, could not be a wife or bear children, and the chances of escape were growing dimmer. Besides, the chief had told her the next time she tried to escape, he could cut off her leg. It was her task to find herbs, roots, berries, and nuts for food, she said, and the tribe gave her freedom to search at will, provided she brought in something each day for the communal pot. It was during her search for early herbs and roots that she had found him, she said, and she had tended him briefly every day but one for the past seven days. Putting more charcoal on the glowing embers, she warned him that he must get well and be on his way before he was found and they both were punished by her tribe. He would be tortured and probably eventually killed, and she would be punished severely. Again, she faded into the darkness, and when Jamie softly called her name, there was no answer.

Jamie slept again; as usual, when he awoke he could not tell whether it was day or night. He was determined to explore the cave, however, and evaluate his suroundings. He could walk with a hobble now, and as he groped around he found his knapsack nearby, with nocake, axe, seed, Bible, and a few nuts all neatly packed and waiting for him. At first Jamie traveled only by feeling the walls of the cave, for he could not see a ray of light. He proceeded, however, hoping he could find his way back to the fire, when he suddenly saw the light at the cave's mouth. When he got to the entrance, he saw evening was falling, and he recognized the place where he had collapsed with exhaustion some seven or eight days before. He ventured no further, however, looking and listening. The tracks were well covered; Jamie guessed that Mary was responsible for making it look as if no one were occupying the cave. Since he was afraid to venture any further, there was nothing left but to try to find his way back to his hiding place, which he accomplished without much difficulty.

Mary did not come that day, and Jamie was waiting at the cave entrance when she appeared the following noon. Her eyes scolded Jamie as she indicated that he must stay hidden deeper in the cave. When they were back at Jamie's bed of skins, and she had given him food, Jamie told her a little about himself. He related that his earliest memories were of being a chimney sweep in London: that Doc Bling had found him, nursed him and taught him; that he had been kidnapped and sold into indentured servitude at twelve; and that he had worked in the tobacco fields almost without incident for eight years. He said that he was called "Jamie"; he was twenty or twenty-two years old, and he simply could not live the rest of his life as a slave or at the whims of men who seemed motivated only by money or great power over other men.

Mary only shook her head and with a flicker of a smile indicated what a foolish young man he was.

She told him how much better off he would have been to have remained safely on the Savedge plantation and lived out his indenture as a peaceful and obedient man. She told him that she had (In what seemed to her a lifetime with the Cherokees) seen many runaway white men captured and that by and large most of them had been tortured (then killed) or simply returned to the owners for a fee. The Cherokees made no secret of the fact that they did not like the white man, but they were quick to recognize the potential value of a possible white runaway slave. The cherokees had pretended to be at peace with the white man since the treaty concocted in 1730 by Sir Alexander Cuming, a Scotsman of South Carolina, but in fact many of them hated the white man, who had brought them veneral disease, smallpox, and liquor. The Cherokees cherished the white man's guns, steel knives, cloth, and looking glasses—and they could not leave the liquor alone no matter how hard they tried—but they knew that the white man ultimately wanted their hunting grounds and wanted to change their way of life. The Cherokees knew how to make war with other Indian nations, but they didn't know how to handle the white man's products, and they wanted him to stay out of their territory.

Each day Mary came and brought him food and water; each day Jamie grew stronger, but he was pale for the want of light, and his muscles began to grow flat and soft. About the end of June, Jamie told Mary that he was planning to strike out again and try his success in crossing the great mountain. Although words were hard to come by, he thanked her with his eyes and an offer of some of his tobacco seed, but Mary declined and asked him not to leave until she had returned again.

Two days later Mary returned early in the morning with food. Jamie saw immediately that she was dressed differently, in moccasins and a short deerskin dress extending only to mid-calf. She appeared very nervous and was constantly looking over her shoulder, as if she thought someone might be following her. Somehow, it was little surprise to Jamie, when he said that he was ready to be on his way, that Mary announced she was going with him. Jamie was not sure what he thought about the new arrangement. Indeed, he liked her companionship and he realized that her knowledge of Indian ways would be invaluable to him, but how could he be responsible for her when he was hard pressed to take care of himself? Nevertheless, Mary's mind seemed made up as she motioned him to follow her up the mountainside.

Mary carried no burden and was well ahead of Jamie, hampered by his knapsack and slight limp, but they proceeded cautiously, and Jamie kept up without too much difficulty. As they came to the ridgetop above the cave, Jamie could see the river winding below; although he could not see the Indian village, he could hear the activity in the distance. At the crest of the ridge Mary took up a pack from a cache where she obviously had placed it day before, and to Jamie's surprise, even with the backpack, she still led him briskly but cautiously along the ridgetop.

All day they kept the river in sight off to their right, and they stopped only briefly to chew some dried meat and dried fruit from Mary's pack (they were saving the nocake) and to sip water from her gourd canteen. The light grew dimmer in the dense forest as the sun began to set, and Jamie had begun to think that he could go no further when Mary indicated that he should take refuge for the night in a huge, hollow log. As Mary disappeared toward the river, Jamie cautiously crept into the tree hollow and was asleep almost immediately.

Jamie didn't know whether it was the sun or the crackle of footsteeps on pebbles which woke him. In any case, he warily looked out and saw Mary standing where he had last seen her. As he gathered his knapsack and gingerly made his way out of the tree, he again detected Mary's extreme nervousness. When she motioned him forward to the base of a huge oak tree, from behind it stepped a young Indian girl— or maybe Jamie thought, it was a white girl in Indian dress. She was younger than he, of medium build and height, with long brown hair and brown eyes.. She was neither pretty nor ugly, but rather she appeared strong, willowy, and healthy. Like Mary, she was dressed in a short deerskin dress and moccasins, and also had a backpack, which apparently she had hidden out beforehand. Jamie was extremely startled and confused when Mary announced very simply that this was

Little Deer and she was going with them. Although Mary did not ask Jamie's permission and approval in words, her eyes and her expression took their place. For his part, Jamie's silence indicated to Mary his acceptance of the situation.

As they proceeded single file along an animal trail, with Mary leading, followed by Little Deer, then Jamie, he sensed that the young girl did not quite know whether or not she wanted to be a part of this venture. Often she looked behind her, and beyond Jamie without actually seeing him, and she was startled at every slightest sound. Thus they traveled very hard for five days, leaving the river and climbing higher and higher into the mountains. Mary spoke to Little Deer in what Jamie presumed to be Cherokee, since it obviously wasn't English. On the sixth day they came upon an outcropping of rock with a spring of water nearby, and Mary indicated that they should rest here for a few days. They had not heard any human sound since leaving the cave, except for that brief time in the vicinity of the Indian village.

Jamie didn't know where they were but did know that they were traveling at a higher elevation than he had ever been, for it was harder to breathe, and he was more light-headed, than ever before. He caught a brush hen with a snare and Mary cooked it over charcoal from a nearby tree which had been burned by lightening. When he wondered what he was doing in that remote wilderness with two strange women, he quickly remembered that he would not be there at all had it not been for Mary. He didn't know about Little Deer, though. So far she seemed to be a part of the venture only because Mary had ordered her to come. He wondered if the maiden would prove more of a burden than either he or Mary could handle.

It was mid-July, and even in the mountains it was not difficult to find enough roots, edible plants, berries, nuts, as well as an abundance of animals, for food. What began to worry Jamie, though, was whether they would be able to find and store enough food for the long winter that was bound to come. He would not be able to plant any of his seed this summer, for the season was already growing short. He would have to talk to Mary; maybe they could devise a plan.

Near the end of the second day of rest Jamie and Mary both were growing restless, but Little Deer seemed remarkably complacent and uninvolved. Jamie broached the subject of future plans; since he had no knowledge of the country into which they were headed, he wondered if Mary did. She seemed pleased that Jamie was consulting her, for she had been on the verge of bringing up the same subject. She spoke in English, which Little Deer appeared to understand a little; when the girl looked puzzled, Mary often halted and explained in Cherokee. For the first time, the maiden seemed to show some interest and become part of the group.

As she stirred the embers, and now and then glanced at Jamie as if seeking approval, Mary began by explaining why she had brought Little Deer along.

She reminded Jamie that she had long wanted to escape the bonds of the Cherokee because she knew there was a better life—or at least a different life more to her liking. She repeated that she had practically reared Little Deer, having had virtually full charge of her under the tutelage of the chief. She had taught the child some English, the language of her unknown white parent or parents, and Mary was determined the girl should seek a different life than she herself had lived. She finally had convinced Little Deer that if she did not excape she would become the wife of a brave, only to bear him several half-breed children. Moreover, she would have little chance of survival in the harsh world of the Cherokees, where war was a way of life. Women played a strong role in Cherokee life, and white women were often adopted into their clans, as both Mary and Little Deer had been, but the life of a white woman among the Indians was still very unpredictable. Jamie said nothing, and a flicker of embarrassment played on Little Deer's face, as Mary continued.

She said she had heard the Cherokee stories about the Great Mountain and the huge valleys, rivers, and immense hunting grounds beyond. She had listened in the background as the stories were told of the Watauga Country beyond the Great Mountain, where the soil was as rich as manure itself, and where the forest was so full of animals and the rivers so full of fish that one had much trouble choosing between them. It was said, however, that the waning Muskogean tribes of the Dallas people inhabited many of those great valleys, and it was known that the Natchez and Overhill Indians were seeking to control some of that territory, even as some Cherokees were beginning to push their settlements further into that region. Therefore, the Cherokee tribe, with which Mary had spent most of her life thought it unwise to brave the harshness of the Great Mountain only to face inevitable war with other Indian tribes, or other clans of their own tribe, when for the time being, they had sufficient space where they were.

For Years, Mary had dreamed of escaping to those remote valleys or foothills beyound the Great Mountain in hope of finding refuge, perhaps with other white people hiding themselves away, both from white men who wanted to control them and from hostile Indians. Perhaps there were some few white people who had already found a Promised Land and had built themselves a special way of life, using the hills, mountains, valleys, and rivers to protect that way of life from the impatience of the outside world.

She had heard some of the braves tell of crossing the Great Mountain in much the same direction as the three of them were now headed; beyond, there was a huge lake through which a large river flowed down into the great valley below. That lake and river marked the Watauga Country and it was for that lake that Mary thought they ought to aim. If, according to the stories the braves had told, they could find the lake and river they would have an abundance of game, wild berries, wild grain—perhaps everything they needed for winter. Mary warned Jamie, however, that the Cherokee brave was prone to exaggerate in his story-telling —the lake might be just a wide place in the river— but she had no doubt that the river existed and the abundance of food was real. She had heard too many braves speak of it too many times. Both Jamie and Little Deer were quiet, indicating to Mary that her plan was acceptable; so they began their preparations for sleep and an early rise to start on the trail in the morning.

However, Mary could not settle down to sleep. She feared she was monopolizing the planning, dictating the future of all three, and she had begun to worry about the consequences if she were wrong. Although she knew that neither Jamie nor Little Deer had any knowledge of the country into which they were headed, she herself had only secondhand knowledge, gained from the stories she had heard. But the rivers and mountains had been mentioned so many times that, even with the exaggerations taken into account, she thought she could draw a map of the area. So she called Jamie and Little Deer to consult again, for if she told them what she had heard repeatedly over the years maybe that would make her more sure.

As they gathered again to listen, Mary drew a rough map on the ground (see following page).* She told

*Later Jamie drew that map with pokeberry ink on a piece of bark and labeled the rivers and mountains as Mary told him. Other maps of East Tennessee are contained in Appendixes F and G. The map contained in Appendix G is probably the oldest map of the area, but the river names have been modernized.

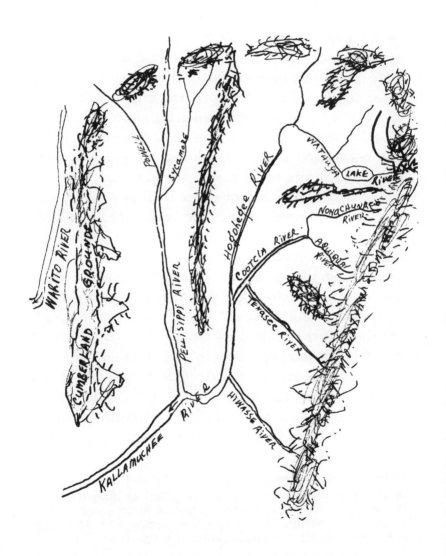

MARY'S MAP OF THE RIVERS WEST OF THE GREAT MOUNTAIN

them she believed they were near the top of the Great Mountain (she marked their location with an x); within about two weeks they should find the head of the Watauga River; then they could follow it to the lake. They could spend the rest of the summer and perhaps the winter on its shores before following the river further down into the valley. She pointed out, further, that her idea of a natural hideaway was far up the Pellissippi River in the remote valleys and hill-country area that both the white man and the Indian seemed to bypass (see Appendixes F and G). The Indians, according to the stories she had heard, were concentrated mostly along the Kallamuchee, Hiwassee and Tenassee rivers, south of the Cootcla River, and sent only occasional hunting parties up the Pellissippi, which they considered their own private hunting grounds, protected on the north, east, and west by mountains and guarded by them on the south. The white man had no reason to enter the area to trade, and only a few Indians hunted there. She had heard the chief tell of sitting in council with the Overhills at Chota on the Tenassee River. He had told many stories of the white man's fear of the Great Mountain, which resulted in his usually entering the Kallamuchee River valley by a route south of that great mountain range. Since the white man's only reason for coming into the area was to trade with the Indians, he was not interested in the remote region up the Pellissippi River; considering it more profitable to trade with the Indians who lived at the south edge of that secluded area, he directed himself south, or around the Cumberland Territory, to more fruitful land beyond. Since rivers were the best travel routes, Mary advocated following the Watauga River, then going south along the Hogohegee, past the Cootcla and Tenassee to the Pellissippi, which they would follow far north into the foothills, where they could hope to find a hideaway forever.

Now, she asked, was her plan still a good one? Both Jamie and Little Deer were very quiet, until Jamie asked whether they would travel, by walking, or by using canoes or rafts. Mary speculated that in the months—perhaps years— to follow, they would do all three. Jamie also asked why they didn't head directly west, across the next mountain range, to find the Pellisippi. Mary replied that they should follow the rivers because their only knowledge of the area came from her map drawn from memory, but if they ran into opposition from Indian tribes, they might have to strike out without its guidance. Anyhow, she would rather explore the valley to some extent and verify where the Pellissippi really was; otherwise they might never recognize their Promised Land when they found it. The quiet which followed signified approval.

They were on the trail before sunrise the next morning. Jamie could tell that they were climbing still higher in elevation as they skirted many beautiful bald meadows to prevent the possibility of being seen. Trees were scarcer now, and great outcroppings of rocks towered above them as they passed, single file, through saddles in the mountains. On the fourth day they began to descend into what they believed to be the Watauga Valley, and from the various vantage points the distant mountains, valleys, and river lay before them in an ageless panorama of beauty. Although they could see a small river in the distance, winding through the foothills and around an occasional taller peak, however, hoping it would lead them to the great lake which was their intermediate destination. For another week they kept to the ridges, with the river on their right, fearful of traveling the river itself lest they be detected. Too, it was plain that, even if they had a canoe or raft, the river was too rough to navigate as it tumbled between high cliffs and through deep gorges, and dropped down dozens of falls hundreds of feet high.

One night, having come close to a bend in the river, they made camp near a peaceful pool where fish abounded and deer and raccoons frolicked in the water on the opposite bank. In this quiet setting Jamie tried hard to figure how the river, seemingly flowing west-by-north, could negotiate the higher mountains which appeared to loom before it. However, when Jamie reproduced in his mind the map that Mary had drawn, he could see that so far she had been right. The river was quiet here, but just around the bend below them they could hear it rumbling down still another cliff.

For another week they kept to the hills, with the river to the right; then late one day they topped a low ridge to see the river flowing peacefully into a small lake. It was not the huge lake described by the Indian braves, but nevertheless it had the semblance of a lake or wide, quiet place in the midst of a wild river. It was the most beautiful scene that Jamie had ever viewed, and he almost cried at the joy of apparently having reached their target. They hastened to find a temporary campsite where they could rest and tomorrow begin a systematic exploration of their new environment; for Mary was sure they were on the Wautauga River and that this was the lake for which they had been aiming, even though the Indian braves' tales had made it seem much larger. Looking across the body of water to the north, they could see that it was not a mile wide at this point; but because it was both a lake and a river, they could not determine how far it extended east and west. Since all of them referred to it as *the lake,* without question or argument, the subject of its identity was never brought up again.

The next morning they held a council to ascertain the main objectives of their search that day. Mary thought they should look for the most heavily used animal trails near the lake, for they would probably indicate the natural route between water and the nearest salt lick. Jamie thought they should look for a cave as near the lake as possible. Little Deer said nothing, as usual. They split up that day for the first time. Mary travelled nearest the lake, Little Deer travelled two hundred or so up the mountainside, and Jamie searched still further from the lake, but keeping it in sight. They were to meet at the lake just before dark to discuss their findings. That night Jamie told of discovering a shallow cave and crossing many animal trails, but finding little else of significance. Little Deer had crossed many animal trails and found some patches of berries, but little else. Mary was elated, having come upon patches of berries, wild fruit trees, and thousands of wild birds along the lakeshore. They decided to search for another day before choosing a permanent campsite. The second day a larger cave was found, and a more abundant supply of game, berries, and fruit were discovered. They decided to settle in the second, larger cave, which was about two hundred yards from the lake; a heavily used animal trail nearby indicated a salt lick further up the mountain. They agreed that they would have to be very careful about making human trails. They would avoid leaving the cave by the same path each time and always be on the lookout for any sign of Indian hunting parties. A stroke of luck occured when, on the third day of occupancy, they discovered a second entrance to the cave. Thus, when they had settled in, Jamie's quarters were near the first entrance, and the women's were near the second. They arranged a system of signals to be used if anyone should sight strange objects or hear strange sounds, and they agreed that the cave would never be totally vacated.

From the standpoint of survival, enjoyment. and lack of interference from external forces, things went very well for the trio during the remainder of that summer of 1740. They killed only enough deer to provide meat and skins for bedding and clothing; Mary made Jamie moccasins, breeches, and a shirt from the deerskins. They saved the nocake they already had on hand and lived on the plentiful berries, roots, wild fruit, nuts, game, and fish. Everything they did pointed toward winter survival, for they knew that this high in the Great Mountain the winter would be harsh and long. They dried deer meat, fish, wild berries, and fruit in the sun; they stored tubers and roots in the coolest parts of the cave. They found and harvested wild corn and cane, and laid away a plentiful supply of nuts.

Often all three visited in the middle part of the day on rainy days, usually in Jamie's part of the cave, and the conversation almost always centered on two subjects: better understanding and knowledge of each other, and their chances and hopes for survival. They discussed at length their plans for living through the winter, their sketchy knowledge of the country into which they were headed, and their hopes of avoiding all humans. Mary made it clear that Jamie, as the man and the chief of their little clan, would make the ultimate decisions, even though she felt privately that her knowledge of ways and her grasp of the geography of the great valley beyond was their only real salvation.

E. LESSONS IN HISTORY

The three struck a bargain that in the days, weeks, and months to follow each would tell the history of his or her life; they would endeavor to explain how they felt, and what they thought about themselves, other persons with whom they had associated, and the world in general. Jamie felt somewhat trapped into the bargain, believing that the women had agreed upon this plan in order to learn more about him. As he thought about the idea, however, he found that he didn't care even if that were the case; rather he welcomed the chance to tell his life story and explain his personal philosophy. Also, he definitely wanted to know more about them. He had never been allowed, or forced, to explain about himself and his ideas, and he wondered how the words would come out when he spoke them aloud rather than thinking them. He knew his feelings, but he was not sure he could make them understand.

The women asked Jamie to begin the procedure, after all had agreed that, while questions would be permitted, highly personal ones would not require an answer. They agreed also that this baring of the soul would serve both as a device for becoming intimately acquainted with each other and also as their entertainment during rainy days and the cold days to come. Fine days must be utilized for gathering and storing food for the winter, making the cave more livable, and planning for the venture to come in the spring. Already, Jamie had begun to think about a raft or boat to float them down the river when they resumed their travels.

As the blazing fall colors adorned the mountains, most of the days were beautiful, clear, and bright, and the three enjoyed the beauty and freedom of the forest and river. By late September, however, the days began to be noticeably shorter, and there was an occasional rainy day when none of the trio left the cave. It was early on one of those rainy days that Mary and Little Deer went to Jamie's quarters and asked him to begin telling them about himself.

Jamie knew that Mary always carried a small pouch with her, and on this occasion he noticed her taking from it a long rawhide string and tying a knot in it. When he questioned her about it, she showed him how she kept account of the days and the months,. She tied a small knot for each day; every new moon she tied a double knot. In the pouch she also carried a stick, into which she carved a notch at the end of a year. Later, she was to use those items in telling her life story.

Jamie began by saying that, the best he could figure, he was now twenty years old, having been born in London of unknown parentage about the year 1720. He omitted the fact that his name at birth might not be *Jamie* at all. He well remembered the days of hunger and drudgery in an orphanage where there were hundreds of other children like him. He also remembered almost as if in a dream now, that he was taken out of that orphanage and forced to climb through chimneys and sweep the coal soot clean. He also rebered that he was forever hungry and cold, and his master often beat him. Those were the days that were so difficult to recall; he explained that it was probably human nature to wipe unpleasantries from the mind and remember only the best, most pleasant things. He told how he ran away from his master when he was about eight and how he roamed the streets of London for weeks; how he became ill and almost died before Doc Bling found him and nursed him back to health. As he told Mary and Little Deer about Doc Bling, tears of happiness came to his eyes at the joy of remembering so wonderful a man. He told them what a great and learned man Doc Bling was but emphasized that most of all he was a wonderfully kindhearted man who believed that every person had a right to his own individuality, responsible to no one but God and himself. Jamie declared that all he now knew, or felt, or thought, and his ability to think things through for himself he owed to the facts that Doc Bling had taught him.

Jamie told of the three wonderful years he had spent with Doc Bling, recounting that Doc had taught him to read and write, encouraging him to think, explore, and decide things for himself. Doc had made him understand that a human, though a mammal, was a different kind of mammal because he could think, plan, and then put plans into action. Doc had been remarkably knowledgeable about the world, its history, and the destiny of mankind; Jamie promised to share with them Doc's knowledge and ideas as best he could; then that knowledge would be theirs as well as his. Some day he would tell them about Doc's death, and about the year he had worked for a physician, but now he wanted to tell them about the part of Doc Bling that lived on in him.

Both Mary and Little Deer were greatly surprised but very happy that Jamie could read and write, and they were astonished at his immense knowledge. At first Jamie was very self-conscious about talking about himself and displaying his knowledge, for he felt that he was lecturing them,but soon he got the knack of making it all sound like a tale of adventure. The two women hung on his every word, too awed to ask questions.

Jamie dropped into his lecturing almost as if he were Doc himself. Indeed, he could almost hear Doc's words repeating the familiar facts as he began by saying that no one really knew how long people had lived on the earth, but that historians knew it had been thousands of years. Civilizations had flourished and disappeared, most records had been lost, but some remained, books were written, and somehow knowledge was passed on to surviving peoples. Records of those ancient times were probably eight or ten thousand years old, and the people were perhaps of a different race, or many races. The story of white man's civilization as we know it, however is contained in the Bible (here Jamie took the tattered copy from his knapsack and showed them), and is supplemented by the writings of the early Roman and Greek civilizations, about two thousand five hundred years ago. From that time we can trace with accuracy the history of the white European, Jamie told them, but there are differing philosophies about how the American Indian happened to be where he is. Doc had thought they were decendants of an earlier civilization, before the history of the white man; Jamie quickly added that the little he knew about their culture led him to agree that before the coming of the white man to the American shores, the Indian way of life, which included acting according to his own conscience, relatively free from greed, was very close to the way Doc Bling had felt all mankind should strive to live.

Nevertheless Jamie went on, while the entire history of the world and its people may not be clear to us, it does seem clear that the destiny of the world today lies in the white man's hands; that is reason enough for us to try to understand the history of the white European and how his world got into its present mess.

Jamie again took the Bible from his knapsack, slowly unwrapped the leather covering it, and very slowly began reading a few passages from the Old

Testament:

"In the beginning God created the heaven and the earth . . . . And God made two great lights; the greater light to rule the day, and the lesser light to rule the night; he made the stars also . . . .and God said let us make man in our image, after our likeness; and let them have dominion over . . . all the earth . . . . and called their name Adam . . .

He then flipped to another part of the Old Testament, saying as if still reading, "And God made woman from Adam's rib, to cleave unto him as his wife and to be as one flesh."

Jamie read again, seemingly without searching, but rather where the Bible fell open, "Behold, I will send my messenger, and he shall prepare the way before me: and the Lord, whom you seek, shall suddenly come to his temple, even the messenger of the covenant, whom ye delight in; behold, he shall come, saith the lord of hosts."

At that point Jamie picked up a large wild pumpkin which he apparently had been saving for the occasion; he told Mary and Little Deer to think of this as the earth, except that the world was many, many thousands times larger, of course. He had drawn lines on the pumpkin to represent the Old World and the East, in relation to western Europe, Africa, India, and the oceans; he showed where they were now, almost exactly opposite that part of the world where Christ was born and where the Romans and Greeks lived and taught so long ago. Jamie, seeing that they were wide-eyed and disbelieving, plunged on before they had time to ask him questions which he might not have been able to answer.

He folded the tattered Bible, wrapped it again, and returned it to his knapsack. At the same time he explained that, as he understood it, the Old Testament, the part of the Bible from which he had just read, was the history of a four thousand-year-old civilization from which sprang the three great religions of Judaism, Christianity, and Mohammedanism, or Islam. Although there is much evidence that the creation story and early parts of the Old Testament were songs and stories transmitted orally until finally, much distorted and slanted to suit the occasion, they were written down about 1200 B.C. Nevertheless, the white western European who calls himself a Christian takes this Bible literally the history and teachings of "God's Chosen People," from whom sprang Jesus Christ, in whom they believe their salvation lies. Doc had explained that the Judeans had designated themselves the "Chosen of God," claiming to be a peculiar race, but in fact, through their intermingling with others over a period of more than four thousand years as they continually struggled to establish Jerusalem as their homeland, they had become a mixture of Asian, Oriental, Egyptian, Assyrian, Armenian, and dozens of other racial extractions.

Jamie pointed out that for the most part, the white European believed that about two thousand years ago God became disenchanted with his so-called Chosen

People, who had strayed far from his laws and teachings, and had sent his only son, Jesus Christ, to the world to teach all his followers how to live and love one another in such a way as to inherit God's plan of salvation and eternal life. However, Jesus was denied by the Judeans, branded as an impostor, and put to death by the Romans, the leaders of western civilization at that time. Although he died in disgrace, our present calendar reckons time from the approximate date of Jesus' birth: according to Doc, the man of letters, "A.D." means "in the year of the Lord."

The Judeans did not accept Christ and the new philosophy; continuing their old ways and teachings, they became almost forgotten. The new faith, Christianity, spread rapidly over the Roman world and was embraced by the white western European as his religion. Jamie digressed briefly to note that Islam also sprang from this common heritage, when about six hundred years after Christ a man named Mohammed established a new set of principles for the Moslems, who considered themselves decendants of the original Judaean tribe. Today, these three great religions exist side by side, but the fact remains that by 1740 the most prolific of the three, the white Christians of western Europe had become the experimenters, explorers, and leaders of the world.

Picking up his narrative, Jamie said that northern barbarians —pagans and idol worshipers—invaded the civilized west and toppled the Roman Empire. Kings established themselves as rulers in Europe "by the grace of God," often governing in conjunction with popes, heads of the Roman Catholic church. That church exercised great power over the people, the rulers, and the law. For many years no man could call himself king in any part of western Europe without the sanction of the pope. Then, just prior to the year 1,000 A.D., Otto the Great deposed a pope, appointed another in his stead, and declared himself king and Holy Roman Emperor. After that time the temporal power of the pope waned. Still, the pope ruled the spiritual lives of most western Europeans, because as head of the Roman Catholic church he dictated all the laws of marriage, divorce, and absolution; and his interpretation of how to attain eternal life was final. As a result, the feudal system of the Middle Ages caught the middle classes between the king and his mobles, who demanded obedience in earthly matters, and the pope, who demanded obedience in everything pertaining to religion.

Jamie went on as if quoting a memorized speech; to a large extent he was doing just that; he was repeating the history that Doc had reviewed for him so many times. This system of dual authority went on, he continued, for about fifteen hundred years (to the end of the Middle Ages), with the white European calling himself a Christian and living according to the rules of the Roman Catholic church. They spread throughout western Europe, where his civilization absorbed northern barbarians. As he had mentioned before, those were the times of feudalism, when the king and a few of his strong nobles owned everything and ruled the lives of the common people, allowing them only barely enough material goods to live; meanwhile the pope, head of the Roman Catholic church, and his emissaries dictated the laws, declared the meaning of the Scriptures, convinced Christians that, since he was the only possible mediator between God and Man, he was the only gate to heaven. Nevertheless, the western white men's society flourished and they quickly became the leaders of the world.

Meanwhile, the Moslem Arabs, the Seljuk Turks, and other eastern peoples had been introduced to the religion of Islam by Mohammed. They occupied a vast geopgraphic territory of the world called the Near East, including the eastern shores of the Mediterranean Sea; they made sweeping conquests into Africa and western Europe, but were stopped short of wholly conquering Europe. However, they continued to occupy some parts of that continent and all the older part of the world, including the birthplace of Christ. As long as Arabs were incontrol of the Moslems. pilgrimages of western European Christians to Christ's birthplace were tolerated. About the year 1,200 A.D., however, the Seliuk turks displaced many Arab leaders in the Moslem world and began to curtail the white westerners' visits to the Holy Land. The Crusades resulted as the pope induced thousands of Christian Western white men, women and children to undertake a series of military expedititons to recover the Holy Land from the Moslem infidels. These Crusades lasted for more than two hundred years and attracted people from all social classes. The feudal nobles saw them as an opportunity to acquire fame, riches, land, and power; in contrast, the misery of the common people was so great that they welcomed any reason to exchange hunger, poverty, and oppression for adventure in the Golden East. More than fifty thousand people took part in the Crusades, which failed to wrest the Holy Land from the infidels, but succeded bringing about great intellectual and social progress by placing the white man of western Europe in contact with the more progressive East.

Also, during the Crusades the wealthy western white man grew accustomed to adding zest to his diet with eastern spices, wines, and fine bread, most of which came overland to the Near East from the Indies, then were redistributed to western Europe. At the same time precious stones, drugs, perfumes, and many luxuries were discovered by the white western Europeans, and who distributed them throughout western Europe by Italian and German merchants. Soon Spain and Portugal, the greatest naval powers of the world at that time, who were being denied access to the Far East, began to search for a direct ocean route to the Indies in order to share in that great wealth of trade.

About that time, other important things were happening, such as the invention of the printing press and the rediscovery of many ancient arts, as well as the revival of man's interest in learning about himself.

More books became available, more people learned to read, and more people began to assess their relative place in society. More people began to learn something about medicine, physics, astronomy, and science. For example, it was discovered that the world is round, that it is not the center of the universe, but revolves around the sun, and that there are other planets like the earth. People began to believe that the earth contained vast lands and waters which were unknown to white western Europeans, and they set about to find them. In all this, the greatest motive was greed for wealth and power.

By 1487 the Portuguese had reached India by a very long ocean route around the continent of Africa, and in 1492 a man named Columbus, sailing under the flag of Spain, made a daring voyage into unknown waters and discovered this continent. Thinking that he had reached India, he called the people here Indians. From that time to this—almost three hundred years now—the white man has steadily taken from the Indian.

The white man found that the Indian knew about tobacco, corn, squash, and dozens of other foods new to Europeans; soon all Europe was craving these things more and more. As a result, white men from many western European countries began setting up colonies and trading posts here in order to trade the Indians European items of beads, cloth, knives, and guns for the Indian goods which Europeans wanted; furs, tobacco, and certain foods. Spain, Portugal, France, and England all laid claim to this part of the world, regardless of the fact that it belonged to the Indians already here, but in a rather short time England got the upper hand, established colonies, and began sending people—a great part of them bonded servants—to populate them.

About that time, also, a great mass of the people of western Europe began to question the claims of the Roman Catholic church. Since they protested, they were called "Protestants," and they established competing Christian churches for the first time. It was King Henry VIII who caused England, as a nation, to break away from the Roman Catholic church. In the 1530s, when he wanted to divorce his Catholic wife and the pope would not give him permission, he established the Church of England, which since then has become one of the strongest critics of the Roman Catholic church. The past two hundred years had seen people throuthout the earth protest against the claims of the Roman Catholic church, set up their own churches, and go to great lengths to find a place in the world where they could worship (or not worship) as they pleased.

Again pulling the Bible from his knapsack, Jamie told them that this translation, commissioned by King James I of England in 1611, is the Authorized King James Version of the Holy Bible, the one which most white western non-Catholics accept as their own. When the Protestant faith was accepted by the English masses, the established Church of England was strengthened, eventually leading to the church and state becoming one and the same. Soon, however, many Englishmen grew weary of such monopoly and wanted to reform or purify the church of England from within. These people, known as Puritans, were among the first to come to the American shores seeking a place of religious tolerance. The Church of England prevails today, but from time to time the king and the parliament have been Puritans, thus aiding in establishing Puritanism in America. Many missionaries have tried to impress their religion upon the Indians, and they all had seen the resulting confusion and chaos as the Indian had tried to choose between his own and the white man's religion.

Jamie looked sheepishly from Mary to Little Deer, wondering how much they had understood. Aware that he had been lecturing largely to Mary, for Little Deer could not have possibly understood, he was just a little sorry that he had preached to them most of the day. He apologized, but still maintained that some background of the greed driving force, and dogmatic religion of the white man must be understood in order to grasp the basic reason for the white man's being in America; actually, the search for religious tolerance was a minor issue when in fact most of the colonies were owned and controlled by Englishmen whose sole motive was to exploit the American land and people by shipping everything they could back to Europe.

Jamie promised to lecture no more that day; the next time he would tell them of his coming to America, his plantation labors, and the reasons for his being where he was today. They parted for the night and Jamie lay back with his hands folded under his head, thinking.

The next few days were beautiful, and the trio busied themselves harvesting and storing for the coming winter, for each fall day was shorter and the nights longer and colder.

Almost a week later, as a slow rain made the brilliant leaves fall from the trees, Mary and Little Deer again appeared early in the morning at Jamie's quarters and asked him to continue his story. Jamie faltered and sputtered a few minutes, asking if Mary should not begin this session. Both women insisted, however, that Jamie continue—it was obvious that they wanted to hear about his personal life—so Jamie quietly began.

He couldn't recall many details of running away from his master when he was about eight years old, but he could vividly remember being cold, hungry, and miserably fevered, eating out of garbage heaps, and sleeping in boxes in the London alleyways; then one day he woke up in the house of a man who called himself Doc Bling. He tried to tell them of his initial shock in finding someone who actually thought of him as a person, giving him a new identity, teaching him to read, write, and think. How happy they had been together, just doing things for each other! They had lived in a very austere manner, using Doc's small amount of money and gathering as much of their own grain as possible. He tried to impress on Mary and

Little Deer that those were the three most wonderful years of his life—a time when he forgot that he had ever existed before—a time of new beginning and a new understanding. He recalled then his sadness when Doc slowly deteriorated and died, and how he went to live and fetch for the physician friend of Doc's.

The story of his being kidnapped in the streets of London and being brought to America and sold as an indentured servant was related very briefly. He spoke lovingly of his first years on the Savedge, however, especially of his relationship with Timothy. In the approximately eight years there he had learned everything there was to know about the culture of tobacco. Also, he had learned, through reading the few books he could find and talking to people, that all the American colonies were owned and managed by a very small group of greedy and wealthy men, with the majority of the labor being performed by bonded servants like himself.

Jamie told how he was forced to go to religious services on the Savedge and listen to a minister, who usually was just a man who called himself a preacher, iterpret the Holy Bible to them. When it was discovered that Jamie could read the tattered copy of the Bible which he now carried, it was often lent to him for a few days at a time. He wasn't exactly sure what he believed about God and the teachings of that Bible, but he had never told anyone thus far just how he felt. He surely believed that the Old Testament was a good, even if distorted, history of a small segment of the world population at the time it treated. About Jesus Christ, however, he was just not sure that he believed, as Christianity taught, that Jesus was God's only son, or God Himself, sent to reveal Himself to a handful of people. Surely, that could be true, but he just wasn't sure. Carefully he explained that he certainly believed in God; and also believed that Jesus, Mohammed, and perhaps others, were in close communion with Him. He also believed, however, that he himself was often in close communion with God; and he was convinced that God revealed Himself in making plants and animals grow, in making the sun rise each morning, in making the winter cold for the plants and the earth to rest, in making the rain, and in making the mountains and forests beautiful. Most of all, God revealed Himself through humans by making them capable of thinking, loving, and planning - and enjoying a life of their own design. Throughout this speech Jamie could not resist waving his hands as if preaching, and often tears welled up in his eyes as he endeavored to make himself understood. He declared that it was these beliefs that led him to leave the Savedge, seeking a place where he could make his own life and commune with God as he chose.

The story of his journey from the Savedge and his survival thus far was very short. And, as Jamie told it, for the first time in his life he felt that he was truly God's creature, doing what he wanted to do and when he wanted to do it. Then he said that they knew enough about him; and next time it would be

Mary's turn to tell her story.

Even then Jamie did not tell his companions that he had a few shillings tucked away in his underwear. He could tell them later, if the necessity arose. Actually, however, he had begun to wonder whether or not the money was now really worth anything. Here he was in a strange part of the country where the people might never have heard of the value of a shilling. On the other hand, he knew that if by chance he should contact English traders, the money would be good; so he would just bide his time and keep the money tucked away.

By this time, it was late and the women were making ready to return to their quarters when loud, crashing noises came rumbling through the cave. They were all so startled that they rushed from the cave though Jamie's entrance; then, seeing that darkness was falling, they quickly formulated a plan to determine the cause of the noise. Jamie would take the overland trail to the second entrance while Mary and Little Deer were stealing back through the cave itself. If their worst fears—that they were being attacked by Indians—were true, they planned to scatter and meet two days later at the first cave they had discovered upon reaching the lake.

As Jamie dodged stealthily from tree to tree around the mountain he tried to think what they had done to leave a trail or otherwise cause an Indian hunting party to find them. Because of the unusual precautions he was taking, he knew the women would reach their quarters before he could circle the mountain to their entrance. When he was no more than a hundred yards away, he heard loud growling and groaning sounds inside the cave; then, as though the devil himself were after him, out rushed a huge black bear, almost rolling down the mountainside toward the lake. Jamie ran in to see if Mary and Little Deer were unharmed; he was curious to hear how they had routed the bear, as well as to see what damage the animal had done.

Mary related that she had determined from the growling, scratching, and clawing that the intruder was a bear, which she and Little Deer had put to flight with a pine-knot torch. He had been into their storehouse of winter food, however, and had eaten or destroyed a good part of it. No doubt this was the bear's usual hibernation den; as Mary pointed out, this experience should teach them at least three lessons. First, winter was upon them, because bears did not seek places for hibernation until winter was actually beginning. Second, since the creature might return, either they would have to move or continually be on guard. Third, a large part of their winter's supply of food had disappeared with the bear.

They decided to remain in the cave and try to keep the bear scared away by guarding each entrance at least until he had relocated himself in a new den. Unfortunately, they could do little about replenishing the lost food supply until spring. Food was the real worry. A charcoal fire in each entrance probably would keep the bear away, but even a charcoal fire could be smelled for miles, making discovery more likely if anyone came near.

In the next few weeks the trio doubled their efforts to gather nuts and roots, but the fruits and berries had vanished with the season. Ripened persimmons were about the only fruit to be found, and there was no known way to preserve them. It was plain that they would have to ration the remainder of the stored food and depend to a larger extent than they had expected on game and fish. Through all this Mary was cheerful, that they would survive the winter in fine shape if they planned properly.

The first snow was falling as the trio met near the middle of the cave for safety, and Mary began the saga of her life. Apparently the bear had found another winter home, for they had not seen him again, but they kept the charcoal fires burning just the same.

At first Mary was apologetic for her slowness of speech—her constant halting and searching for a word or thought—and her lack of Jamie's vocabulary. After he had reassured her that she should speak in her own way, and even stop and explain certain things to Little Deer in Cherokee, she seemed more at ease and began her story. Although Jamie was eager to hear, Little Deer seemed for the first time to come alive as she hung on Mary's every word and thought.

Mary told them that she was born the sixth child in a family of four girls and three boys in Aberdeen, Scotland, about 1700, which made her forty years old give or take a year. Her father was a cooper, making and repairing barrels and casks for a living. The income of the family was meager, however, and they were very poor because her father was not a thoroughbred Scotsman in ancestry, but rather a descendant of a Spanish sailor who, having fled in the defeat of the Spanish Armada in 1588, had chosen to remain in Scotland and marry a local woman. Therefore, he was commissioned to do work of a cooper only when a full-blooded Scotsman could not be found to do it.

The family was very poor both materially and intellectually. Neither father and mother nor any of the children could read or write, for such was not the mode of the times. Mary worked in her family's trade from as early as she could remember; after she was six or seven years old, when there was no work with barrels and casks, she was often sent to beg on the streets. Their house was a hovel on the edge of Aberdeen where there never was enough food or clothing.

When she was thirteen or fourteen years old, Mary was sent to work in some sort of factory, where she worked sixteen hours a day turning a grinding wheel to sharpen tools. She was allowed to rest very little; at first often whipped and chained to the bench for not producing enough work, she almost died from the sheer drudgery of the labor, but within a year the toil had hardened and made her very stong and muscular, and better able to tolerate the work. She received no pay, for somehow her father owed the factory owner for raw materials. Eventually when the debt was not being paid off quickly enough, it was suggested that

if she were turned over to the factory owner as a bondservant, the debt would be canceled. How reluctant
her family was to give her up, Mary did not know,
but it was done. Very shortly thereafter she found herself on her way to America, having been sold or traded
as a bondservant like any other commodity.

So it was that Mary came to America as a bondservant to an Englishman who owned a plantation in
the Albemarle Settlement (now North Carolina).
She was then about sixteen, a year younger than Little
Deer was then. She had grown strong and muscular
from approximately three years' work in the tool shop
and felt that she was destined for the fields as a
laborer. However, when she reached the plantation,
she was told that she would be a house servant; when
she tried to tell the owner she knew nothing about
such work, she was told that she could learn. The crux
of the matter, she soon learned, was that "house
servant" also meant "mistress" to the plantation
owner.

Mary was at the plantation about six years; during
that time she learned to cook, sew, and mend; sometimes she was called into the fields because she was so
muscular and strong. The plantation owner was not a
kind man, and she was often beaten if she displeased
him, sometimes for no apparent reason. She was his
mistress at his will and pleasure and was not allowed
to associate with any other men on the plantation.
During those six years she bore three children, all boys,
but each was taken away when he was about a year old,

and she never saw them again.

Her master, whose name, Drummond, was also that of the governor of Albermarle, gradually became engaged in trading with parties of Indians who first came to the plantation to exchange deerskins for knives, guns, cloth, whiskey and trinkets. Rather quickly, Mr. Drummond began to organize trading routes and to travel with his wares into Indian territory. At first he took only trusted menservants in his trading parties, but soon he began to take Mary along. She never knew exactly why she was included, but always felt as if she were on exhibition. Soon she began to learn some of the Indian language, although she was never allowed to join in the converstion or trading.

It was on one of those trading ventures that the son of an Indian chieftain abruptly asked to buy Mary for a wife. She was quickly sent away out of earshot, so she could not hear the terms of the trade, but in the end she learned that she had been traded. She was about twenty-two years old, she said, when she became the second wife of Long Knife, son of the chief.

With head downcast and displaying unusual emotion, Mary tried to explain how she felt in that strange new world. She lived in the cabin with Long Knife, his wife, and two sons, but to her surprise she was, for the most part, ignored. She was given tasks and was not mistreated, but neither was she included in anything. The actions of those around her plainly showed that she would neither be a true wife to Long Knife nor even, perhaps, a part of any tribal activity until some family matter was settled. Gradually the children began to talk to her, and ask her to play with them; this led to Long Knife's first wife, Wilani, to address her occasionally.

It was well over a year before Wilani openly accepted Mary as her sister and part of the clan, who called her Meli (Pronounced "May Lee"). By then, Mary had learned a good bit of the Cherokee language, and Wilani began talking to her and explaining things to her. She had decided to accept Mary as her sister, allowing her to be second wife to her husband, Long Knife, who would become chief of the tribe soon because it would be proper for a great chief to have two wives. The rites of accepting Mary into Wilani's clan and adopting her as her sister were carried out at the August harvest festival or Green Corn Ceremony; following that, a very simple ceremony made her Long Knife's wife. During the next twelve years, she bore him three sons; however, they were not recognized as Mary's own children, but rather as children of the family, and Wilani was head woman of the family.

Mary was blinking her eyes very hard to keep from openly crying as she recalled those unhappy days. Quickly, however, she recovered, announcing that at this point she had best tell Jamie—and Little Deer, too, if she didn't already know— what she knew about Cherokee history.

The Cherokee Nation, she began, is made up of seven clans with names which, loosely translated, mean Bird, Wolf, Deer, Paint, Blue, Long Hair, and

Wild Potato. Marriages are permitted only outside the clan. Poligamy is permissible but not universal, and divorce is a matter of mutual consent. There are no courts or magistrates or police; so each clan enforces the unwritten law of an eye for an eye, a tooth for a tooth, and a life for a life, and if a guilty person flees from punishment, a kinsman is required to take his place.

The Cherokees live in about eighty towns, connected by well-blazed trails, most of which are near the headwaters of the Tenassee and Hiwassee rivers; their central government seems to be in Chota, a town somewhere on the Tenassee River. Cherokee towns vary in size from a dozen up to two hundred houses; the average is probably about a hundred. Each town is made up of members of the various clans. The council house, or temple, is on the west side of a central square, where dances and ceremonies are held; around the council house are grouped the houses and gardens. Each family has a cabin built of solid logs caulked with clay and roofed with bark and branches. Some of the houses, like those of the Yuchi Indians, are either wholly or partially underground. Each has a small scooped-out fireplace in the center of the floor; beside it is a large, flat rock, or hearthstone, for baking cornbread. One end of the house is used for storage of food and other family possessions, and the other is for sleeping. Beds made of saplings and wooden splints are attached to the walls. When a house contains an under ground area, it is used for winter living, and where they sleep during cold weather. That part of the house is furnished spearately, even with a separate fireplace where, during the cold months, a fire is kept burning all day and is banked at night.

The Cherokee council house is a combination temple for religious rites and public hall for civil and military councils. It is a seven-sided building, because of the seven clans of the Cherokee Nation, and members of each clan sit only in their own section. The sacred number seven also is repeated in the number of pillars, tiers, and official seats for tribal officials, as well as in many other appointments she could neither remember nor understand. Near the center post of the temple a fire burns and is never allowed to go out.

Basically, Mary explained, the Cherokee people are farmers, and although they have some domesticated animals like cattle, horses, and dogs, they hunt wild game for most of their meat. Corn is their main crop, but they also grow beans, gourds, pumpkins, squash, and sunflowers, whose seeds are ground into' meal. Their many varieties of corn all fall into three basic types; "six weeks" corn, which is small-grained, ripens in about two months, and is roasted in the milk stage; "hominy" corn, which has smooth, hard kernels that may be red, blue, white, yellow or any combination of colors; and "flour" corn, which has large white kernals and is the most important of all. Corn is literally the "staff of life" to the Cherokee and is the subject of dozens of myths and rituals. The Cherokee people perform magical rites at every stage of its growth to insure its welfare and abundant production. The Cherokee name for corn is *tsalu*, but the name of the spirit of corn is *Agawela*, or "Old Woman". According to Cherokee legend, when Agawela was killed by her sons, her body brought forth corn.

In addition to cultivated plants and domesticated animals, the Cherokee make great use of nature's wild fruits, nuts, mushrooms, fish, crayfish, frogs, bird eggs, and dozens of insects such as cicadas. In late winter and early spring, before new crops come in, food is often scarce, and survival sometimes hangs on eating the bark and roots of trees.

The Cherokee call themselves *Ani-Yunwiya*, "Principal People," and they are said to be the largest single tribe anywhere near here (see Appendix H).* They have a dim tradition of their ancestors' having come to this land as part of a long-drawn-out mass migration in which the Delawares, and Algonquin tribe, formed the vanguard. Due to their leader-

---

*Samuel Carter says that some believe the Cherokees to be one of the ten lost tribes of Israel: others believe they crossed the Bering Sea and drifted to the Appalachians; still others think they are linked to the South American Indian. However, he says, even in DeSota's time, they occupied approximately 43,000 square miles in North Carolina, Georgia, Tennessee, and Virginia in some sixty town or villages generally located in mountanous sections; the population was estimated at 25,000. Samuel Carter III, *Cherokee Sunset* (Garden City, New York: Doubleday & Company, Inc., 1976), p. 16.

ship, Cherokee tradition says, the Delawares are the grandfathers of all Indians, and the Cherokee themselves are uncles of the Creeks, Choctaws, Chickasaws, and brothers of certain other tribes, undoubtedly the Iroquois and Tuscararas. The tradition goes on to say that, just before or after crossing a great body of water, the tribes separated, some going south and some north. Present-day chiefs, however, say that the Indian migration legend tends to telescope time, simply because it has been handed down from one generation to the next by word of mouth.

Cherokee craftsmen are especially proud of their hand-carved stone pipes, pottery, and wood carvings. A good craftsman can form beautiful and distinctive designs on pottery, ceremonial masks, and drums hollowed out of buckeye trees. Many objects used every day, such as dugout canoes, are carved of wood. These canoes are made from poplar trees that are hollowed out by alternately scraping and burning. Although some of them are nearly forty feet long, two feet wide, and about a foot deep, they are not excessively heavy because the remaining wood is only one to two inches thick—and poplar is light weight, yet strong.

They also excel in weaving beautiful multicolored baskets and mats from narrow strips of cane which are dyed in brilliant colors. For special purposes, they make garments of wild turkey feathers which are practical and warm without being bulky. Headdresses are made from the feathers of eagles and the white crane.

Although the Cherokee use the tomahawk and the axe as a weapon, their most important one (before the coming of the white man), was the blowgun. It is about eight feet long and made from a hollowed-out reed or cane. Small, slender, wooden darts tufted with thistle-down are blown from it with enough force to kill small game and birds. It is said that other Indians use a blow-gun also, but none are as well made and as accurate as those of the Cherokee.

Cherokee clothing is simple and practical, Mary said. The women wear short skirts and shoulder mantles (or short vests), like her own and Little Deer's, and the men wear breechcloths and sleeveless shirts. In winter, of course, they dress warmer, but in the same type clothes, most of which are made from deer-skins like these (she pointed to their own clothing). Both sexes wear moccasins that are made like short boots, reaching about halfway up the legs, like these (she pointed again), but when the men are in the forests in cold weather and on hunting trips they wear deerskin leggings like loose trouser legs; she promised to make Jamie some of those for winter. The men are beardless by nature and are suspicious of bearded men like Jamie. Often they keep their heads shaved of all but a decorative crown piece, and some of the braves dye and tattoo their skins. The women keep their hair long, plaited in wreaths, and tie it in a tight knot behind, like hers and Little Deer's, she said.

The religion of the Cherokee is rather simple, in

that they believe there is a Great Spirit, but if there is a God, then He is not a single personality but rather He is everyting around them; that combination makes up the Great Spirit. They believe that the Great Spirit loaned them their land, the animals, and all natural things they need, and they themselves own nothing but the man-made improvements on the land. They humanize all nature, believing that rivers, rocks, trees, birds, animals, and the stars in the heavens are equally alive. Long Man River is a giver of life; his waters, when they perform the rite of "going to the river" every morning, cleanses the flesh of sin and sickness. The bears are people who could talk like everyone else if they wished, but they wisely choose to keep silent. If a Cherokee is obliged to kill an animal for food, his first task is to ask its forgiveness. There are no priests, as such, in their religion, but they do have both medicine men to combat illnesses and help with difficult decisions and conjurors to bring rain when needed or make a warrior invulnerable in battle. Even the conjurors, however, are no match for the Raven Mockers who swoop through the air in fiery shape with arms outstretched like wings to rob the dying man of life.

The religious organization seems closely tied to the civil government, and all who hold governmental or religious positions are dedicated in childhood to their future place in the tribe undergoing special training in history, rituals, beliefs, medicinal formulas, and fasting. Dances form a great part of Cherokee religious ceremonies, and their festivals are a principal diversion also. They have the Green Corn dance in the August harvest season; they dance before going to war as well as to celebrate their return; they dance to greet visitors; and they have many social, often humorous, dances named after birds and animals wherein they imitate hunting the creatures or their mating.

In the Cherokee society the family is the most important unit, and the mother's side of the family is emphasized. All children belong to the maternal clan, and members of each generation throughout the clan consider themselves to be brothers and sisters. Within the family, inheritance of position, privileges, and prerogatives are passed from the mother's brother to his nephews. Relationships on the father's side are recognized, but they are considered less important. Therefore, every Cherokee has a close tie to four of the seven clans—the mother's, the father's, the paternal grandfather's and the maternal grandfather's— and every person is expected to marry into one of the last two.

There always had been much intertribal warfare, Mary explained, but mostly it consisted of hit-and-run raids against traditional Indian enemies such as the Creeks, Shawnee, Iroquois, Catawba, Yuchi, and Delawares rather than long wars designed to wipe out entire tribes.* It was on their return from such a raid,

* "Their principal occupation, as William Fyffe had noted in the eighteenth century, was making war—against the Creeks to the south, or the Choctaws to the west, or any other tribe handy to their borders. Fyfe was struck by the Cherokees' method of

when Mary's second son was a baby, about 1725 or
1726, that a number of hostages were brought in;
among them was a baby girl about four to six months
old. Long Knife was gradually assuming the duties of
chief of their village because his father was growing
old; so it became Wilani's choice of adopting the baby
into her clan or putting her to death. When Wilani
chose adoption, the baby was placed in Mary's care to
suckle and nurture. Named Little Deer, she was often
referred to as Mary's child, because most of the tribe
believed Little Deer part white and part Indian. Her
heredity did not alter Little Deer's acceptance into the
clan, tribe, and village, however, and she held a place
of great honor in the family. Mary declared, as she
placed her arm around Little Deer's shoulder, that she
soon came to love her more than all three sons she had
borne, and she used every trick to be alone with her as
much as possible. She was permitted to teach Little
Deer English and from the beginning, Mary said,
she felt the attachment was mutual. At that, an unusual
show of emotion for a Cherokee maiden, Little Deer
snuggled up to Mary and put her arms around her.

fanning a militant spirit among the young, teaching them not
only combat skills but courage, endurance, and indifference
to pain. If courage, was sometimes confused with barbarity,
there were other consequences of this schooling. Like the early
Viking of Scandinavia, the Cherokees learned to honor their
warrior forbears. No Indian tribe in Norty America became more
dedicated to the land which held their father's graves. Sacred
soil. Inviolable earth'' (Carter, *Cherokee Sunset, p. 19).

Mary had talked on for most of the day, with both Jamie and Little Deer spellbound. Plainly, the story must end for the time being, but Mary promised, before they parted, that next time she would tell how she felt about religion and perhaps one's relations with other people; then she would help Little Deer tell her story.

The bad weather held, and that first snow lay more than twelve inches deep before it stopped two days later. Mary and Little Deer were occupied for almost a week in making snowshoes and in showing Jamie their use. When the storytelling did resume, they all had snowshoes on which to travel when they were forced to venture from the cave.

After the bear's raid, they had made a survey of the remaining food supply, and Mary was rationing it very strictly. She figured that if spring would not be too late, they could survive in good shape. Besides, each had a little nocake in reserve which they did not count since they were saving it as a last measure against starvation.

It was not until early in December that the trio met again to hear the rest of Mary's story. First Jamie reminded Mary that she should finish by telling what she thought about God and religion. She began by saying that she had never heard the history of the white western European as Jamie had explained it, but it had opened her eyes to an understanding of many things about which she had always wondered. For example, why did most white men think themselves better, and more authoritative on most matters, than anyone else in the world? She understood for the first time that people had to learn to be greedy, seeking power, wealth, and position, and many white men had taught themselves well. She admitted that she missed the ways of her own people because in her early youth she had been admonished to fear God, to worship Him, and to believe in the Bible, although she had never been told why. Even though she had missed her own people and had tried to escape from the Cherokees, in her eighteen years with them she had experienced a new religion and a different view of God.

The sacred number seven was a vital part of the life of all Cherokees, she explained. They believed that the universe was sevenfold, with seven heavens and seven directions—north, south, east, west, above, below, and the center where they lived. Seven clans were the cornerstone of their social organization, and seven great ceremonies, recurring regularly, formed the circle of their religious life. They believed in one supreme being, *Yowa*, but the name was too sacred to be spoken aloud except once a year by special priests dedicated from childhood. *Yowa* was thought to be the unity of three beings, "The Elder Fires Above," who had created the universe—the sun, the moon, and the world. Then *Yowa* had returned to the seventh heaven and left the sun and the moon to finish the creation of all stars and living things and rule over them. During the creation process, the sun and moon had appointed fire to be man's protector and his go-between with the sun. Smoke was the fire's messenger, bearing man's prayers from earth to heaven. The moon controlled religious rituals, and its phases dictated dates for beginning and ending ceremonies. There were spirits to symbolize the four points of the compass. East was a red spirit that gave power in war; north was a blue spirit indicating defeat; west was a black specter of death; and south was the white spirit of peace. Most things in nature such as thunder, animals, plants, and water were believed to have spirit counterparts. The mountains and forests were peopled with fairies who were friendly when undisturbed, but played tricks on you when offended. Ghosts and spirits of the dead hovered around their former homes before finally departing for the other world and its seven heavens. There were seven ceremonies held periodically; six of them were held every year and one recurred every seventh year. *

Mary explained that she believed a great part of the Indian philosophy; she also believed that the Holy Bible which Jamie carried could certainly be true, and she had no quarrel with it, except she could not understand how the writers could proclaim themselves the sole religious authorities in the world. On the other hand, as a poor, ignorant woman who couldn't read,

*Thomas M. N. Lewis and Madeline Kneberg, *Tribes That Slumber* (Knoxville: The University of Tennessee Press, 1958), pp. 175-76.

she could only base her thoughts and feelings on what
she had seen and heard in her lifetime. Looking at
Little Deer as if to ask forgiveness, she confessed she
couldn't believe in all the Cherokee ritual and ceremonies. What she thought and felt, she guessed,
would fall somewhere between the beliefs and practices
of the white man and the Cherokee. Looking at Jamie as
if pleading for help, she assumed she believed as
he did as much as anyone ever could, without being
Jamie himself. She believed there was a God, a Supreme Being or Creator, and that He revealed himself
through the processes of life and death, the love of one
person for another, the mountains, the animals, the forests, the rivers, the snow, and the ability of mankind to
think and plan. She had a definite concept of God's—
or nature's—laws, and she had a definite feeling when
she was keeping or breaking one of those laws. She
believed there was a life beyond the grave, but she
hadn't figured out whether it was free or she had to
earn it. She believed everyone would be in eternity,
but some would be happy, while others less fortunate
would be alone, separated from the happy ones. Like
Jamie, she felt that she maintained a closeness with
nature—or God—or the Supreme Being, and no one
had to tell her how.

When she had finished, Jamie put out his hand and,
for the first time, touched Mary, squeezing and strok-
inng her hand as if to assure her they were kindred
spirits and that they were as one, through their understanding of each other.

Suddenly it was Little Deer's turn. As Mary took her hand, she looked afraid and confused, but slowly she began, speaking in halting English, with only a smattering of Cherokee words here and there. She claimed that, although she knew only Meli as her mother, for there had been nothing in her life to make her believe differently. Meli had taught her to speak English, but she had not taught her any of the white man's conflicting ways and religion. While Little Deer had understood most of what Jamie had said, it was a strange new world of ideas, and she preferred to maintain the simple ways and religion of the Cherokee. Appearing braver and more forward as she continued, for the first time she looked directly at Jamie and admitted she had been pursuaded to come on this venture only because of her love for Meli and the latter's promise of a better and happier life. How life could be happier and better than it was in their own village she couldn't understand, but Meli had told her that it would be so. Now, she blurted with a woebegone face and downcast eyes, she wished that she and Meli were back in their own village and that Jamie had never come along.

F. WITH THE CHEROKEE INDIANS

That winter of 1740-41 passed slowly for the trio. There was hardly a day before April that the bare ground could be seen through the snow. For days on end none of them left the shelter of the cave, for there was no need to brave the snow and risk being tracked back to their hideaway. Their supply of grain, dried berries, fruit, and nuts began to grow short by March, but there was plenty of meat to be had for the taking. Snaring a rabbit or a wood hen in the snow was fairly easy, the plentiful lake fish could be speared through the ice with a long pole, and more than once Jamie killed small deer with rocks and sticks. Long before they had any need of it, Mary had gathered the bark from certain trees for the three to eat for rougage. All in all, they managed quite well, considering the fact that the bear had deprived them of much excellent food which they had labored so hard to store away.

By April the snow began to melt in spots, the ice on the lake grew thinner close to the shore, and here and there early hardy plants could be seen peeping through the dead leaves and snow. Mary assured them that from then on they would have no more food problems, for in addition to the new plants they could also find last year's nuts hidden among the fallen leaves. With the few tiny green plants, nuts, and meat, they would have an abundance of food. Besides, each had a bit of nocake in reserve, for that last possible desperate moment before starvation.

As rapidly as winter turned to spring, just as rapidly did their plans turn to the venture down the Watauga River in search of the Hogohegee. Although there was not much discussion about going, it seemed to be understood by Jamie and Mary, at least, that as soon as the ice on the river cleared and they felt that enough food could be foraged along the way, they would set out. The decision would be chiefly Mary's; since she was the most experienced, Jamie was more than willing to take her advice. Little Deer was quiet as usual, indicating that she would do as Meli wished.

April showers had come and gone when in early May and their knapsacks were packed and ready, Mary decided they should be on their way. All three were eager to set out again, after the winter confinement, but Mary warned them that their bodies would have to be retempered by traveling short distances the first few days, gradually working up to longer, harder treks. As they continued to parallel the south bank of the Watauga River, it was soon obvious that they were rapidly descending in altitude. The dense air became much hotter and harder to breathe; they could see more abundant wild flowers and greenery and game and fish were always plentiful.

It must have been the latter part of June, by Mary's reckoning, when they reached the confluence of the Watauga and a larger river which flowed in a generally southerly direction. According to Mary's memory and the map she had had Jamie draw and label, they had only to follow the Hogohegee south, past the confluence of the Cootcla and Hiwassee rivers, to reach the point where the Pellissippi flowed from the north into the Kallamuchee. From there they would go far north into the valley of the Pellissippi to seek their Promised Land. Now, according to Mary's map, they should cross the Hogohegee River and travel south along its west bank; thus they would avoid crossing not only the Cootcla and Hiwassee but also any other streams arising in the Great Mountain as they flowed west into the Hogohegee and Kallamuchee. They still would encounter numerous streams to be crossed, even ones flowing into the Hogohegee and Kallamuchee from the west, but according to Mary's information, there were many more rivers flowing from the east than from the west. The immediate problem was that the Hogohegee was a wide, wild river, dangerous to cross at that point; in all likelihood it would grow wider, rougher, and harder to cross further south. Therefore, they had three choices: backtrack and cross the Watauga; go further north along the east bank of the Hogohegee to find a crossing place; or simply travel south along the east side of the Hogohegee with the hope of finding a crossing place further downstream. In her haste to be on their way, Mary advised the latter course; Jamie agreed, and Little Deer, as usual, expressed no opinion.

By mid-July they had found a place to ford the Hogohegee with only a minimum of swimming; so they were now on target, heading south along the west bank of the river. Food was plentiful with wild fruit, berries, and grain beginning to ripen. Also, signs of human habitation began to appear here and there: a mark on a tree, a moccasin print, and once a distant sound which might have been a dog's bark. Those signs, which suggested the likelihood that soon they would encounter groups of Cherokee, led them to plan their strategy if they ever were visitors, willing or unwilling, in a Cherokee village.

With just such a possibility in mind, they made every effort to see themselves as the Cherokee might see them. Here was Jamie, a white European and a declared Englishman, a fact which should be in his favor; Little Deer, obviously a Cherokee maiden, could pass for Jamie's wife; and out of the blue they were inspired to designate Mary as Jamie's older sister. They would say that Jamie and Mary were from a wealthy English family, had come first to Virginia, then to North Carolina, seeking a new way of life and religious tolerance. Having become disallusioned with the white man's ways, however, they had decided to travel, trade, and live among the Cherokees. They would declare that they had spent some time in Mary and Little Deer's village on the other side of the Great Mountain; there Jamie had fallen in love with Little Deer and married her; now she was not only Jamie's wife but also a sister to Mary. Mary would tell them her chief's real name, hoping that any Indians they met would not know the chief of such a small village so far away. Would all this sound logical to the Cherokees? Mary hoped so; Jamie wasn't sure; and Little Deer was willing to call herself Jamie's wife if Meli thought it best. After thinking the plan through a number of times, Mary stated her only reservation concerned the way they could prove themselves wealthy Englishmen, able to travel at their will and pleasure. It was then that Jamie disclosed that he had a hoard of twelve shillings which he could produce one at a time to prove their wealth, provided the Cherokee whom they might contact knew the value of a shilling. Anyway, since they could think of no better plan, the die was cast.

They stayed well back from the river but tried to keep it in view in order to maintain direction; however, dense undergrowth was so fiercly troublesome to deal with, sometimes they were days traveling only a few miles. In early August, as they approached the confluence of the Hogohegee and Cootcla rivers, they saw on the bank an Indian vllage, with patches of corn and small vegetables nearby. They camped on the west side of a small ridge, made no fire, and were contemplating whether to hail the occupants of the village, when about noon they were paid a visit by about a dozen Cherokee braves.

There were no signs of hostility as they openly greeted each other, exchanging handclasps. Jamie introduced his party just as they had planned, using Little Deer as interpreter. Of course, Mary would have been a better interpreter, but they didn't know how the Cherokee would react to Mary's being able to speak Cherokee while her brother could not. The braves told Jamie that they had been sent by their village chief to invite them to visit in peace, talk, dance, and perhaps trade. When Jamie accepted, they all headed toward the river.

Crossing the river in three dugouts, they landed just at the edge of the village square. It seemed to the trio that the whole Cherokee Nation had turned out to greet them, when in fact it was only the occupants of a village of about two hundred houses. Nevertheless, they were welcomed with great ceremony and seated in a place of honor in the village square where dancing and feasting were begun immediately. In about half an hour the chief and his wife, along with seven other older men of the tribe, joined them in a circle. There were nodding, handclasps, and bowing all around, but no words, except the chief's saying, in perfect English, "Welcome to our village." As the feasting and dancing continued, the visitors were presented gifts of eagle tails and beautiful shells. Long bronze pipes of tobacco were passed around the circle, and each man smoked in his turn as Mary, Little Deer, and the chief's wife sat with arms crossed, looking straight ahead. Each visitor was brought food by a beautifully dressed young Indian maiden especially assigned to serve only one.

This went on until just before dark, when, the dancing having paused, the chief rose and spoke slowly but in good English. He said that he was Atta-kullakulla, friend and confidant of the Great White King George II, and that all white men, especially Englishmen, were welcome in his village. They would enjoy the feasting for yet a while, and the next day they would talk at length and tell many stories. Chief Attakullakulla then went around the circle and wel-comed each of the trio with a typical English hand-shake. At dusk, they were taken to a cabin which had been prepared for the visitors to spend the night. As far as they knew, the dancing continued until dawn.

The next day the trio were seated in their places of honor as guests; the same leaders formed the circle of honor; and the dancing and feasting continued much as before. Late in the afternoon the drums and the danc-ing stopped. Chief Attakullakulla arose and faced the four cardinal directions of the compass in turn: then the elder in the circle, obviously the conjuror or medicine man arose and threw something on the fire, sending great puffs of smoke toward the sky. Only then did Chief Attakullakulla begin to speak. Again he told them that he was Attakullakulla, once known as *Ukwanequa*, or "White Owl," and that he was one of the greatest of all the Cherokee chiefs. He said that, although his braves had told him who the visitors were, the village had known of their coming for weeks, having watched them travel the west bank of the Great River: the Cherokee had known that the bearded one came in peace, for he carried no weapon and brought his women with him. The Chief told them that many years ago an English or Scottish man named Sir Alexander Cuming had smoked the peace pipe with the cherokee, trading them many useful goods in the name of the Great White King George II; furthermore, he himself, along with six other Cherokee chiefs, had traveled to England to visit the great King and his people. Attakullakulla told them that the seven Cherokee chiefs had laid a crown of possum fur at the feet of the king, who in turn gave them many gifts of cloth, guns, gunpowder, bullets, knives, and iron kettles. Now, Chief Attakulla-kulla told them, the Cherokee lived in peace with the white Englishmen to the east, welcoming them as traders who possessed many things that the Cherokee wanted and cherished. He told them that although it was true that the white man had taken some of their land and had brought them many diseases, he still believed that the Cherokee and the white man could live together in peace. Besides, the French traders to the west, who even wanted to take Chota, their capitol, from the Cherokee, were far worse than the English; so the English white man and the Cherokee must unite as brothers. He confided that Englishmen to the east, like the great trader James Adair, had agreed to barter with them, help them build forts, and befriend them at all costs. Chief Attakullakulla then sat down, indicating with a bow that it was Jamie's turn to speak.

Jamie was learning quickly that he must act un-afraid, talk slowly, with much waving of the hands, and pretend to be the most knowledgeable person in all creation, if he were to impress Chief Attakullakulla. As he arose in the center of the circle, he bowed gracefully to the chief, his wife, and the seven Chero-kee elders. With a great show of pomp, he opened his knapsack and removed the Holy Bible. As he showed it to each one in the circle, he explained that this was a record of the God of the English people; he, whom they called *Tsemi,* * would read some of it to them, and then they would pray to the God of the white man to make them all brothers and bring them peace forever. Jamie began the story of creation in Genesis, reading just enough to impress the Cherokee with his learning; then, with the Bible held above his head, he prayed that peace and plenty be poured out on Chief Atta-kullakulla and his people. As he concluded he could see that the Cherokee were indeed impressed; so he re-peated his well-rehearsed story once more, describing how he and his sister had left England, then the east, seeking a haven among the great Cherokee people. He said they had lived for more than a year with a small tribe of Cherokee across the Great Mountain; there he had fallen in love with Little Deer and had married her; and now having been so wonderfully guided by the Great Spirit, they had found this mar-velous village where they could sit in peace with a great

*Jamie's name in Cherokee is *Tsemi;* since the "T" is silent, the pronunciation is "Semi."

Cherokee chief and his people. Jamie showing them a shilling, boasted that he had a great deal of English money to buy whatever the three needed, but their needs and wants were few indeed. They were searching for a place where they could live in peace and harmony with the Great Spirit, with each other, with nature, and with the Cherokee. They had heard stories of a great river known as the Pellissippi and their goal was to go far up that river or one of its tributaries, where no white man dwelt, and to live in peace and brotherhood with all mankind. Pointing to the Cherokee peace pipes, Jamie then told Chief Attakullakulla that he had both the seed and the knowledge to grow the most wonderful tobacco in all the world, and the tobacco which he would grow would be his specialty in trading with the Cherokee. Then he sat down.

Attakullakulla nodded that he was pleased and Mary smiled sweetly at Jamie as Little Deer finished her interpretation and also sat down.

The remainder of that day the trio were entertained with games. A special ball game, something like modern football or lacrosse, was called "the brother of war." Here two teams opposed each other on a two hundred-yard sanded field with goals at each end. The object was to get a small deerskin ball stuffed with hair across the opponent's goal. They also played a game called *chungke,* which involved rolling a smoothly rounded stone disk while two players ran after it with long poles; as one player tried to knock down the stone with a thrown pole, the second player attempted to down the first pole with his own. The winner was the one whose pole was nearest the stone when it stopped. There was much gambling on each throw, and it was a lively game indeed.* Just before dark the games ended, and the trio went to their cabin for the night.

On the third day they gathered again in the honor circle, and after a brief ceremony Attakullakulla invited the visitors to remain in the village for the celebration of the Green Corn Ceremony, or August harvest festival. Each of the guests recognized the invitation as a great honor, and even though Jamie and Mary wanted to be on their way, they knew that failure to accept it would surely invoke suspicion. Therefore, Jamie arose slowly and deliberately, and with much bowing and ceremony he graciously accepted Chief Attakullakulla's kind invitation. Jamie even ventured to say, on the spur of the moment, that he now considered himself a brother of the great chief of the Cherokee, Attakullakulla, because their innermost thoughts and philosophies of life were so much alike.

Chief Attakullakulla explained that the early, or "six weeks"'' corn, was then ripe enough to eat, but eating the new corn was forbidden until after the Green Corn Ceremony. He had already dispatched seven messengers to gather seven ears of corn, each ear to be picked from the field of a different clan.

*Alberta and Carson Brewer, *Valley So Wild,* Knoxville, Tn.: East Tennessee Historical Society, 1975), p. 24.
p. 182.

When the messengers should return with the corn, the chief and his seven counselors would fast for seven days (the day of return and six more). Meanwhile, his people were already assembling, and the ceremony would begin on the seventh day. The sacred fire would be extinguished and rekindled as before, and already, the chief explained, the sacrifice was being prepared. For the sacrifice, deer's tongue and kernels from the seven ears of corn would be used, and he would dedicate the corn to *Yowa* as he offered a prayer of thanksgiving. Then he would place the corn and the deer's tongue in the sacred fire and sprinkle a miracle potion, consisting mostly of powdered tobacco, over them. Meanwhile, food prepared from the new corn would be served; that is, everyone except the chief and seven counselors, who could eat only the corn from the previous years' harvest for yet another seven days.*

The three visitors bided their time and in their own ways enjoyed the honors being bestowed upon them; Jamie was finding everything new and of great import; Mary was relishing perhaps for the first time, the feeling of being a person worthy of honoring; and Little Deer, as usual, was rather noncommital.

At the conclusion of the Green Corn Ceremony, Jamie approached Chief Attakullakulla in private,

*Thomas M. N. Lewis and Madeline Kneberg, *Tribes That Slumber,* (Knoxville: The University of Tennessee Press, 1958), p. 180.

for by now they usually could converse well enough without an interpreter, and told the chief that with his permission, the three wanted to be on their way up the great Pellissippi Valley before winter. Attakulla-kulla said that the next day would be one for telling stories, dancing, and feasting; only such an occasion would suffice to send his new friends on their journey.

They gathered at noon in the village square and, after Chief Attakullakulla had boasted of his great storytelling ability, he entertained them with one old Cherokee legend after another.* He began with the Cherokee version of creation, describing how *Wasi* had received the laws, how he had struck the rock in the wilderness and produced water when his people had dug with stones without finding it; how their tribes had wandered many years in the desert; how they had crossed a great sea by grapevines to escape their enemies; how great serpents had visited upon them until many of their tribes died; and how a pillar of cloud by day and of fire by night had been sent by the Great Spirit to guide them out of the wilderness and into this great land. As Attakullakulla spoke, and all the people of the village listened as intently as if they had never heard the story before, Jamie was struck by the parallel, in almost every detail, of this story with that in the Old Testament. According to

*Robert Lindsay Mason, *The Lure of the Great Smokies,* (New York: Houghton Mifflin Co., 1927), p. 262.

Attakullakulla, the ancient Cherokee also had their Ark of the Covenant, behind which priests of the tribes marched, and they possessed traditional records, transmitted orally from generation to generation, of the Deluge, which destroyed every living thing except a chosen few. Attakullakulla told his own version of these stories with great imagination and a wealth of detail. After almost two hours of telling religious legends, he told his version of other Cherokee stories such as "The Rabbit and the Tar Baby," "The first Fire," How They Brought Back Tobacco," "The Race between the Crane and the Hummingbird," "The Origin of the Bear," "A Witch Tale," "Daughter of the Sun," and many others.*

The storytelling went on until just after dark, when the chief said he would finish with one other story, newer in origin, which he personally knew to be true. Then he revealed that about two hundred years before, great-grandparents of elders of this very village saw the coming of a white man, DeSota, who brought with him many velvet-clad, steel armored strangers with skull-colored faces.† The strangers brought no women, but using their horses and guns they killed many of the Cherokee, calling them barbarians and refusing their usual courtesies of proffered food. Finally in a great battle that continued many days, the Cherokee had captured six of DeSota's men and driven

*Carter, *Cherokee Sunset,* p. 6.
†Masonpn, *op. cit.,* pp. 262-96.

Desoto and the others out of their land and toward the great Mississippi River. Ordinarily, the six captured men would have been put to death, but they proved themselves inventive and ingenious in teaching the Cherokee new ways, such as making and using strange weapons, that the great Cherokee chief of that time had given them wives and had banished them to a region far up a branch of the Pellissippi River. Over the years black slaves and white renegades had been known to escape the white man in the east and find shelter among that group, which by Attakullakulla's time had grown to a village of thirty or forty houses (see Appendix I for author's version). The Cherokee called that group *Melungos*— the very name by which DeSoto himself designated a great number of his men. Over the years, the Cherokee considered them neither friend nor foe however, since trade and other contacts between them were frequent; all those who knew anything about the *Melungos* considered them to be under Cherokee protection.*

Attakullakulla assured Jamie that he and his women were free to leave the next day, and start their journey up the Pellissippi, suggesting that they might like to seek that group of *Melungos* which he had described. Then, as if the thought had struck him that very moment, Attakullakulla promised to send a dozen braves to

*Jean Patterson Bible, *Melungeons Yesterday and Today* (Rogersville,: East Tennessee Printing Co., 1975), p. 11.

transport them in dugouts, exploring the Pellissippi region and maybe even visiting the *Melungos*, if the trio would agree to return the braves before the Great New Moon Ceremony and spend the winter in his village. On the spur of the moment, as well, Jamie accepted with all the graciousness his newfound ways would permit, and before the three retired, he presented Attakullakulla with a shilling which the well-traveled chief, fully aware of its value, gratefully received.

Mary, confused and unsure about the turn of events, did not tell Jamie that she feared he had made a wrong decision. Rather, when they were alone for the night, Jamie and Mary discussed only whether to seek and join the *Melungos*, or simply try to find a separate place in which to settle. Finally, they agreed to let Attakullakulla braves show them where the *Melungos* lived, explore the area as they had planned, return to the village for the winter, and definitely decide where to settle before setting out again the following spring.

Thus it was on a midmorning of late August 1741 that Jamie, Mary, and Little Deer set out with twelve Cherokee braves in three dugouts canoes. They headed south along the Kallamuchee River, planning to travel north up the Pellissippi. The weather was perfect, and the wild beauty of the river and the surrounding area was incomparable to anything they had ever seen. After they had headed north up the Pellissippi the going was slowed at times by the necessity of carrying the canoes around waterfalls and rough, unnavigable water. At other times, they would forge for days as the experienced braves sent their canoes skimming along at a good speed, even against the current. Near the end of September they left the Pellissippi River to head up a smaller river which the braves called the "Waters of the Sycamore". The third day up the Sycamore the braves informed Jamie that if they wanted to go further, they would have to go on foot; the Indians said that the *Melungo* tribe lived about four or five days' travel further north, at the edge of the mountains.

They camped for a week, roaming the low hills and valleys as they explored the country around them. Mary figured that they were just west of a small mountain which ranged from north to south along the western shores of the Pellissippi River. Through their discussions with the Cherokee braves and from their own observations, they learned of another, smaller river just west of them called the Powell, and definitely there were higher mountain ranges to the north. This was indeed the area Mary often had referred to as their "Promised Land"; there was no doubt about that. The soil along the creek bottoms and up the narrow valleys was rich beyond anything they had ever seen before—surely it would grow anything they could want to plant—and wild game, fruits, berries, and nuts were plentiful. They could find no more perfect place, guarded as it was on the south by the friendly Cherokee and on all other sides by virtually impassable rivers and mountains. By the end of September, they began their return trip to Attakullakulla's village.

They were welcomed as before with much dancing and feasting, but on the day after their return, when they again gathered in the honor circle, Attakullakulla arose looking stern and harsh. He announced that during the trio's absence he had been visited by a messenger sent by Chief Long Knife from across the Great Mountain; Chief Long Knife demanded the return of his wife and daughter, as well as the death of the white bearded one. Attakullakulla went on to say, however, that in his great wisdom, and after many days of deep thought, he had returned a message to Long Knife that the bearded white man was now a brother to the Great Cherokee Chief Attakullakulla, and that the three deserved to live in peace as friends and equals to the Cherokee rather than slaves and subordinates. Also, he told Jamie, he had promised Long Knife that the bearded one would send him English money with which he could buy many knives and guns. Then he sat down.

With this Jamie arose and presented Attakullakulla with a second shilling for himself and two shillings to be sent by messenger to Long Knife. He agreed that he and Attakullakulla were indeed brothers, believers in the same Great Spirit, and he told the chief that he and his women would be forever grateful for his tremendous generosity and friendship; so for the time being, at least, the matter seemed settled.

It was early October and, as the autumn leaves began to fall and the new moon appeared, Attakullakulla and his people began to prepare for the Great

New Moon Ceremony. Since this was the season of the year, according to Cherokee tradition, in which the world was created, the Cherokee name for the ceremony was *Nuwatiegwa*, meaning "Big Medicine," but it was commonly called the great New Moon Ceremony. To prepare for it, each family brought from its own fields produce such as corn, beans, pumpkins, and squash. Part of that produce was for the general feast, and the remainder was for the chief to distribute among unfortunate families whose harvest had been meager. On the night of the moon's appearance, the women performed a religious dance during which only infants were permitted to sleep; everyone else kept vigil until just before dawn, when the whole village, including the infants, were assembled by the priest in a long line on the riverbank. As the sun rose and the priest signaled, they all waded into the river and submerged themselves and their children seven times. Previously, the priest had placed a sacred crystal on a stand near the river's edge; so, as they emerged from the water one at a time, each person gazed into the sacred crystal. If the image reflected in the crystal appeared to be lying down, that individual would die before spring, according to Cherokee tradition. If, however, the crystal image seemed to be standing erect, that person would survive the coming winter. Those who felt themselves doomed remained apart and fasted while the others changed into dry clothes and, returning to the temple, feasted on the sacrifice of deer's tongue. The next night was devoted to another religious dance by the women, and again none but infants slept. Just before nightfall of the second day, those who had previously seen themselves lying down in their reflection were taken once more by the priest to the riverbank where the crystal-gazing was repeated. If on the second try a person found himself erect, he repeated the seven submergings in the river and then considered himself safe through the winter. The unfortunates who found themselves, even on the second try, lying down in the crystal image, had one more chance to escape their fate, but that crucial test was deferred until the next new moon, four weeks later.*

Mary had previously told Jamie of a Friends Made Ceremony that the Cherokee sometimes celebrated. Nevertheless, it was a great surprise to Jamie when Chief Attakullakulla announced that in ten days the village would hold such a ceremony to celebrate the bond of eternal friendship between Attakullakulla on the one hand and Jamie and his women on the other. During the ceremony Attakullakulla and Jamie would vow to regard the other as himself as long as they both lived. Mary informed Jamie that the profoundly religious ceremony would symbolize not only the bond of friendship between the two men but also the union of all the people with *Yowa* in purification of their minds and bodies.

*Lewis and Kneberg, *op. cit., p. 182.*

In preparation, seven hunters were sent after game, seven other braves were sent to bring in seven kinds of evergreen plants, and seven more were assigned to clean and prepare the temple. Seven women were designated to fast for seven days in the presence of the chief and his seven counselors. Just before dawn on the day of the ceremony, the seats and vessels of the officials were whitened with clay, and white buckskin was spread over the seats and in front of them, since white was symbolic of peace and purity.

At sunrise all the villagers assembled in the temple to watch the ritual of rekindling the sacred fire, which was fed with seven different kinds of wood: blackjack oak, post oak, red oak, sycamore, locust, plum, and redbud. After the high priest had sprinkled tobacco on the fire and the smoke had risen, he directed the smoke in the four cardinal directions with the wing-fan of a white heron. Then a whitened pottery vessel filled with water was placed on the fire, and the seven evergreen plants dropped into it. That brew of evergreen, composed of cedar, white pine, hemlock, mistletoe, greenbrier, heartleaf, and ginseng, became the medicine of purification that was used on several occasions during the five-day festival.

The second part of the Friends Made Ceremony was performed by seven men who held white sycamore rods. Their purpose was to drive away evil spirits by chanting a sacred formula while they struck the eaves of each building in the village with their rods. While they were carrying out that task, the chief priest dressed in white robes and prepared to sing the great hymn to *Yowa*. When the men with the rods returned, the priest went outside and began to sing, climbing onto the roof of the temple as he sang. The hymn was composed of seven verses, each sung in a different melody and repeated four times; at the conclusion, the priest reentered the temple. Next, the seven men who had driven the evil spirits from the village dipped seven white gourds into the evergreen medicine which had been brewing over the sacred fire. Then each presented a gourdfull of the medicine to the head man of his own clan, who drank from it and handed it on. As the brew passed from person to person, each one drank some and rubbed some on his chest. After everyone had drunk from the gourds, the hymn to *Yowa* was repeated.

The usual ritual of bathing and sacrifice followed, and at sunset the hymn was sung again to *Yowa*. At that point a feast was served, and during the evening that followed, women joined in the friendship dance. Rituals were similar the second and third days, except the hymn was not sung to *Yowa;* on the fourth day the first day's rituals, including the hymn to *Yowa*, were repeated. On the fifth and last day, the medicine basket was taken from the vessel and stored in a secret place, and ceremonies were concluded when the officials and the priest left the temple, saying as they made their exit, "Now I depart." The people followed, holdin their hearts a deep sense of security and peace.*

*Lewis and Kneberg, *op. cit.*, pp. 183-84.

During the winter of 1741-42 Chief Attakullakulla began to refer to the trio as "Tsemi and his brood", which some misunderstood and, whether purposely or not, converted into the term "Tsemi-Breed." Quickly, after that, the young braves—with an eye for Little Deer's youth and obvious appeal as a desirable mate for any young man—jokingly changed the term into "Tsemi's Breeding." Strangely enough, the name stuck, because in later dealings with white men who expected all white Englishmen to have a Christian, or given name and a surname, Jamie automatically used the names, Jamie Breeding, both of which had been bestowed on him by people he loved and greatly respected.

G. FROM 1742 ONWARD

In the early spring of 1742 Jamie, Mary, and Little Deer were laden with many gifts by Chief Attakulla-kulla and his people; presented a dugout filled with much food and supplies; and almost tearfully sent on their return trip up the Pellissippi to the waters of the Sycamore. This time they traveled openly and un-afraid, knowing that they were now under the personal care and protection of a good, peaceful, and powerful chief of the Cherokee nation.

Jamie still carried with him the cane seed which he had taken from the Savedge; Attakullakulla had given him the seeds of squash, beans, corn, and many other edible plants; in addition, Jamie had sprouted some of his carefully hoarded tobacco seed in a small box; and he was tenderly mothering the thirty or forty plants which he was growing in his homemade hothouse. He had promised Chief Attakullakulla to bring him some of that tobacco in the fall.

They returned almost to the exact spot where they and the twelve braves had camped the past fall, for it was here that they wanted to establish their home. After careful thought, they decided to locate their cabin in a hollow just off the creek, out of the path and direct scrutiny of any chance passerby. However, seed must be planted before a cabin could be built, and before seed could be planted, the land had to be cleared. Mary showed Jamie how the Cherokee accomplished that by controlled burning, which involved cutting only a pathway around the perimeter of the prospective field and setting fire to the area. The field of about three or four acres which they had chosen was rich indeed; it was partially cleared, then burned three times before they judged it ready to be planted. Finally, however, by the end of May planting was completed, and a cabin would be started.

A cold, clear spring was located near the site where, just a hundred yards from a vantage point overlooking their field and commanding a view far down the creek, they built their three-room log cabin. Although Jamie was an expert axman, his knowledge of building log houses was extremely limited; so the women's instructions in hewing and fitting logs were invaluable. Many times, however, none of them knew, and the job was done by trial and error. However, when it was finished Mary called it a good and livable house, closely resembling the Cherokee cabins. One room was for Jamie, one was for Mary and Little Deer, and the third was the kitchen and common room. The fireplace with its hearthstone was in the center of the common room, the walls of which provided space for storage. Their plans also included using the bedrooms for additional storage as needed.

A great deal of work was done during that summer of 1742, as the cabin was being built and the crops tended at the same time. Although Jamie tried to do most of the hard labor, he often would come upon his women combining their efforts to lift a large log or other heavy object which he could have handled alone. He frequently chided them for such practices, reminding them that he considered it his job to care for them, but they were stubbornly insistent on "doing their share"—and more.

By fall of 1742 the log cabin was livable, with a door and window opening each covered with skins; abundant food crops had been harvested; fish and venison had been dried and stored for the winter; and Jamie's tobacco was drying in his room. By the end of October he had prepared the canoe for a visit with Attakullakulla and his people, planning to take most of the tobacco he had grown, as well as samples of the best corn, squash, beans, cane, sunflower seed and pumpkin. Jamie and his women were proud of their accomplishments and wanted to show their Indian brothers that they were doing well. Therefore Jamie set out by dugout to visit Attakullakulla's village, telling his women that he would be home before snow fell.

His visit to Attakullakulla and his people was a great success, and although it was unprecedented among the Cherokee to hold such a festival so late in the fall, Jamie and his Cherokee friends celebrated his rich harvest for seven days and nights. Chief Attakullakulla, greatly impressed by Jamie's tobacco, lavished gifts of deerskins and eagle tails upon his white brother. He urged Jamie to bring him as much tobacco as possible the following year, for Attakullakulla could barter the surplus to white traders who came in increasing numbers early each summer. Attakullakulla went on to tell Jamie that white traders from Virginia and the Carolinas continued to use the Carolina Road, entering his area from the south (see Appendix H), but a Virginia trader named Vaughan was reported to have discovered recently the Indian trail known as the "Warrior's Path," which led them down through southeast Virginia, across the Nonachunkee and Cootcla rivers, and into this area from the north, much the same way that Jamie and his women had come. He doubted, such a rugged trail would replace the southern trade route. In any case, Attakullakulla promised Jamie to continue guarding him from the south, telling white traders that no cause would be served by their traveling up the barren Pellissippi.

In the early days of 1743 Jamie returned home and the trio settled in for the winter. Life was easy and pleasant, with little else to do but fetch wood—charcoal when it could be found—for the fire, hunt when meat

*Mary U. Rothrock, ed., *The French Broad-Holston Country* (Knoxville: East Tennessee Historical Society, 1946), pp. 22-23.

was needed, explore the forest occasionally, and in general, enjoy being free. Jamie constantly made improvements on the cabin, mentally planning on expanding it when necessary. Those thoughts, however, inevitably brought on thoughts of children, which in turn led to the thought of marriage. They had, of course, told their Cherokee friends that he and Little Deer were married, but that lie, along with the others, had been discovered long before. Nevertheless, Jamie had the feeling all along that Little Deer expected him to take her for his wife. Too, sometimes Mary led him to think that she wanted him to take Little Deer for his wife, but at other times she seemed happy to leave things as they were; so the subject just never was brought up.

The spring and summer of 1743 saw the trio planting the same patch and preparing an additional field nearby. There was nothing different about that summer, except Jamie had made himself a plow which he pulled like a mule or ox while one of the women held it in place. They worked hard when it was time to work and rested when it was time to rest, and the season and their labors produced another abundant harvest, even better than the year before.

Again, in the fall of 1743, Jamie visited his cherokee friends to show off his good fortune and abundant harvest. The celebration was carried out as before, and again Jamie had a satisfying visit with Chief Attakullakulla. This time, however, the chief asked whether Jamie had a son yet. Jamie's reply was negative, but what he didn't tell the chief was that he had begun to think about that subject a great deal. The chief even had his conjuror bestow on Jamie a magic potion to assure him a son in the near future. Although it was a good visit, Jamie was glad to return in early December and find his women eager to see him and hear of his visit.

In February, 1744, when the trio decided at last to visit the *Melunos,* they prepared for the visit much as Jamie had prepared for his visits with Chief Atta-kullakulla, except this time Jamie was taking his women along. All three had been warned by the Cherokee against using the word *Melungo* which, for some unexplained reason, implied contempt of these strange people. They carried samples of their tobacco and other harvests, some skins, and other trading items. They were six days finding the clan which, just as Attakullakulla had said, seemed composed of thirty or forty households. The trio was most impressed by their observation that the *Melungos* did not live in a village, like the Cherokee, but rather each house was hidden away up a separate hollow. The five or six houses which Jamie actually saw were constructed of logs, much like his own.

The first of the *Melungos* houses that they came upon was hidden away in a hollow just over the ridge from a small creek, and the blue smoke curling from the chimney was the only sign leading them to it. When the trio approached the cabin, the man who came out appeared to be in his early forties; tall and dark-olive-skinned; with long, straight, black hair, he looked something like a Cherokee in his clothing of homespun cloth and skins; he seemed strong, healthy, and alert; but was very uncommunicative. In an old English accent which Jamie never heard before, he asked who they were and what they wanted. Jamie played the same taciturn game, saying that the three were traveling through the area in an effort to find a likely place to build a cabin; then he asked to visit their leader. Not even inviting them into his cabin, the stranger indicated that they should follow him as he strode to the edge of his clearing.

It was just after noon when the four began following an almost undiscernible trail over ridges and across narrow valleys. In every hollow there was a log cabin with signs of small cultivated patches nearby, but their guide, skirting each one, seemed to be headed in a general direction. Just before sundown they came to the edge of a clearing on the brow of a low ridge, and their guide said that their clan leader, Moses Collins lived there. The guide told them to wait until after he had gone in; then Mr. Collins would come out to see them. Sure enough, as their guide later made his way back into the forest, an old man with an oriental-like wisp of beard came around the cabin and greeted them with the same peculiar English accent. His greeting was neither unkind nor friendly, but rather seemed to convey the thought, "You are here, and your are my guests. I will be kind but not friendly."

The old man inquired their reasons for being there, and Jamie answered much as he had answered the guide. Very quickly, however, Mr. Collins told them that he was aware they had been living in a cabin on the Sycamore for the past two winters, and again he stated that he was curious about the reason for their visit. Immediately, the young man answered that he was Jamie Breeding; he just wanted to be friendly, and trade, and get to know the clan as neighbors. Just as quickly the old man asserted that his people neither needed nor wanted any neighbors, and that there was a vast expanse of territory in which they all could live without getting too close to each other. Grudgingly, he said they could spend the night in his cabin, but they would have to be on their way early the next day.

Only five people live in the cabin; Mr. Collins and his wife, a man in his midforties, whom Jamie took to be Mr. Collins' son, and his wife, and a beautiful young lass of about thirteen. They all shared the guide's strange appearance and firmly declined to answer most questions or engage in unnecessary conversation; yet the visitors were afforded all the amenities of food, warmth, and bed. Apparently the *Melungos* did not want to trade, but Jamie did leave Mr. Collins some of his tobacco. The following morning the younger man escorted the trio to exactly the same spot where they had first encountered the first of the clan, then he too mysteriously disappeared into the forest—and there suddenly it was as if they had never seen anyone in the area..

On their return to their own cabin, Jamie and Mary discussed the strangeness of the clan, wondering whether they would ever become acquainted with any of them. Within a few days, however the effects of the extraordinary visit began to wear off, and the three quickly reverted simply to enjoying the freedom and quiet of the great country around them.

One late March day 1744, Jamie asked Mary to survey the planting with him. Pointing out where he thought each crop should be planted, and asking her ideas on the subject, where she thought each crop should be planted, he spent most of a beautiful spring day just sitting with her overlooking their two fields and the creek as it gurgled below them. Mary was quiter than usual and Jamie, more talkative. Toward midafternoon Jamie, who could contain himself no longer, suddenly blurted out that he wanted Mary to to be his wife. Startled by the words, Mary still appeared to have been anticipating them with some dread. Actually, Jamie couldn't judge whether she was happy or just confused by the whole idea. Quickly, however, Mary regained her composure and began to point out the foolishness of Jamie's proposal.

Reminding him that she was old enough to be his mother, she said that he should take Little Deer for his wife, for she could bear him children, whereas it was doubtful that Mary could. She presented many other arguments to prove Jamie's decision unwise, but neither any of her arguments nor the look in her eyes denied that Mary did indeed care for and even love Jamie, or that in her heart she had secretly hoped for this day. Jamie, in turn, understanding the emotions behind Mary's words just as he had back in the cave, knew that her feelings for him were deep as his own for her. Therefore, he brushed aside all further discussion, took Mary's hand for only the second time in their years together and asked her to join him in telling Little Deer.

Their marriage ceremony consisted of a self-proclaimed set of statements to each other, spoken in the presence of Little Deer. Afterwards, it was clear that Jamie was extremely happy and at peace for the first time; Mary though quiet, also showed her great happiness; Little Deer, however, seemed more confused and quieter than ever. That night Mary moved into Jamie's room and the new arrangement was consummated.

The planting, cultivation and harvest of 1744 went well with the trio, and when Jamie visited Chief Attakullakulla and his people in November he told the chief that he was expecting a son in January or February. He neglected to mention the fact that his child would be Mary's rather than Little Deer's son. In any case, they celebrated both his bountiful harvest and his good fortune of being an expectant father. After the celebration, Jamie was eager to return to Mary in order to assist Little Deer get his wife through her pregnancy.

Many times during that winter,—the worst they had experienced thus far—Mary told Jamie how happy she was; how amazing that the age of forty-five she was able to conceive and bear their child; whom she hoped would be a boy who some day would be one of the leaders of this great, new country. Truly, hers was an amazing feat, seldom observed among forty-five-year-old women of that day. However, the fact was that Mary's great strength, endurance, and unusual health, which had served her well since her early days in the factory in Scotland, were rapidly waning. In late January 1745, as the time for the baby's birth approached, Mary instinctively knew that she would not survive the birthing of her seventh child. She kept that knowledge well hidden, however, allowing Jamie's enthusiasm and Little Deer's hope to flourish. The child, a boy whom they named Evans Stone, was born in early February, but Mary could not seem to regain her strength. She died at the end of March 1745 and was buried on the knoll where Jamie had asked her to marry him.

A twofold dilemma confronted the survivors: first, coping with Jamie's terrible grief at losing his beloved Mary; and second, keeping the child alive. Not yet two months old, he had been barely existing on Mary's thin, scanty milk. Strangely enough, it was Little Deer who took charge of the situation, convincing Jamie that the child should be taken to Chief Attakullakulla's village and put under the care of a foster mother, or wet nurse, for about a year. When they had hurried downriver with the starving child, told Attakullakulla the whole story, and presented their urgent request, they were fortunate enough to learn that a young mother had just lost a child at birth. Hastily, a bargain was struck; for a shilling, the fifth of Jamie's original twelve, the woman would suckle the child until he was one year old.

They remained only a few days with Attakullakulla, for they must return to spring planting. On their return plainly Jamie's heart was not in tilling the soil, for he missed his wife and son. More and more he sat looking across at the knoll where Mary was buried, while Little Deer performed the work necessary to grow the crops. Finally, as the fall harvesttime of 1745 approached, Little Deer boldly announced that she was going to accompany Jamie to visit Attakullakulla's people in late October, and that there she and Jamie would be married. After all, she was over twenty years old by then; marriage was long overdue; and Mary would approve. Her surprising proposal didn't arouse Jamie one way or the other, for nothing mattered to him.

After Jamie and Little Deer had reached the Cherokee village, however, and Jamie had seen his son again, and once the celebration had begun, Jamie began to revive a little. Attakullakulla, aware of Jamie's trauma, invited them to spend the winter in his village, where they could be married in grand Cherokee style and then take their son Evans Stone home with them before spring planting time. The wedding took place in December, at the time of the third full moon of the Cherokee new year; the winter passed quickly, but by late March Jamie and Little Deer were eager to start for the Sycamore, to begin a new life there.

Records show that by 1750 Little Deer had borne Jamie a son, then a daughter, then another son. The first son was named James Carpenter, in honor of his father and Chief Attahullahulla, whom the English called "Little Carpenter;" naturally, the daughter was named Little Mary; and Little Deer's second son went unnamed for many months until his mother began calling him Second Son. All Jamie's love was lavished on Evans Stone and Little Mary and he entrusted their teaching to no one but himself; hardly noticing his other two sons, he allowed Little Deer to rear them as she chose.

EPILOGUE

During the following years Chief Attakullakulla kept Jamie aware of the increasing number of white explorers coming into the area and of distant wars and battles, but he and his family remained secluded far up the Sycamore. Stephen Holston, who visited the area about 1748, reportedly changed the name of the Hogohegee River to the Holston. The Cootcla River became the French Broad, indicating "the struggle between the English and the French for control of the eastern part of the Mississippi Valley, of which East Tennessee is a part, and of the early advantage held by the French in that contest." Since it rises near the Broad River in North Carolina and flows westward through the mountains into the French-claimed Mississippi Valley, this was a natural name and it stuck. The French did not occupy East Tennessee chiefly because the English defeated them in a series of wars which were ended by the Treaty of Paris in 1763—a treaty by which the French ceded to England all her land east of the Mississippi.

Throughout this time the English had maintained friendship with the Cherokee, trying to keep their loyalty by building forts for their protection on the banks of the Little Tennessee River in 1756-57. When the Cherokee eventually deserted to the French, they were too late, for English settlers had begun pouring into East Tennessee. The Watauga Settlement was established in 1769, Carter's Valley Settlement in 1772, and the James White Fort (later Knoxville) in 1786. Aver's Treaty of 1777, drawn up between North Carolina (of which this area was a part at that time) and the Cherokee Indians, was not clear concerning boundaries between Indian land and that available to white settlers. At one time the Cherokee were banished to an area north of Greenville, but before he signed this treaty, Chief Attakullakulla made sure that the white signers knew that the land between the Pellissippi and the Powell rivers belonged to his white brother, Jamie Breeding.

In 1783 North Carolina adopted the policy of disregarding Indian titles to the land because the Cherokee had sided with the British in the Revolutionary War. Therefore, all land lying generally south and west of the French Broad River was offered to purchasers on the easiest of terms with little or no actual cash outlay. As a result of this "land grab" act, that part of Tennessee outside the area reserved for Indians swarmed with men seeking land with which to speculate. Even then, however, it was understood that the upper reaches of the Pellissippi were already taken. Besides, repeated so often as to be generally believed was Chief Attakullakulla's insistance that no land in that vicinity was worth anything even if it were available.

In 1784, it is reported, Jamie sent his son Evans Stone to visit the new governor of Tennessee; there he paid seven shillings sterling, placed in trust with the state, to assure that Jamie Breeding and his heirs held title to all the land lying between the Powell and the Pellissippi (now the Clinch) rivers as far north as Virginia. Further, it must be noted that seven shillings sterling were worth many pounds in the inflated paper money of the time.

Evans Stone Breeding is reported to have married a young lady from the Carter Valley Settlement in 1773; he inherited Jamie's estate at the latter's death in 1790. Little Mary is said to have been "carried off" by a *Melungo* man and never seen again; James Carpenter took a *Melungo* bride and Second Son married a Cherokee. It is not certain what surnames James Carpenter and Second Son gave to their children, but it is a fact that Evan Stone Breeding sired many offspring who populated the mountains and valleys of that region from that time forward. Most of them kept to the mountains like their ancestors, using the area for a treasured hideaway as civilization, flowing westward, passed them by. Possibly a few of them went west, of course, but it is a fact that many still live in that Promised Land, much as Jamie and Mary did more than two hundred years ago.

Land titles, notes, marriage records, old personal

letters, and tales handed down from generation to generation indicate that at least one of Evans Stone Breeding's sons returned to Virginia and settled in the Shenandoah Valley near the present West Virginia line. This probably accounts for the lineage researched and recorded by E. J. Breeding and others in Appendix J.

BIBLIOGRAPHY

Barth, John. *The Sot-Weed Factor.* Garden City, N.Y.: Doubleday & Co., 1967.

Bonar, James. *Malthus and His Work.* London: Macmillan & Co., 1885.

Bowen, Ivor. *The Great Enclosure of Common Lands in Wales.* London: Chiswick Press, 1914.

Brewer, Alberta and Carson. *Valley So Wild.* Knoxville: East Tennessee Historical Society, 1975.

Brooks, Maurice G. *The Appalachians.* Boston: Houghton Mifflin Co., 1965.

Buckland, W. W. *The Roman Law of Slavery.* Cambridge: Cambridge University Press, 1908.

Buckley, S. B. "Mountains of North Carolina and Tennessee." Unpublished paper, 1969.

Campbell, John C. *The Southern Highlander and his Homeland.* Lexington: University of Kentucky Press, 1969.

Carter, Samuel III. *Cherokee Sunset: A Nation Betrayed, Garden City, N.Y.: Doubleday & Co., 1976.*

Cate, Herma, Clyde Ussery, and Randy Armstong,

The Southern Appalachian Heritage. Kingsport, Tenn.: Holston Publishing Corp., 1974.

Caudill, Harry M. *Night Comes to the Cumberlands.* Boston: Little, Brown & Co., Atlantic Monthly Press, 1962.

Chamberlayne, Edward. *State of England.* Cambridge: Cambridge University Press, 1669.

Chase, Richard. *American Folk Tales and Songs.* New York: Dover Publications, 1971.

Clark, Joe. *Tennessee Hill Folk.* Nashville, Tenn.: Williams Printing Co., 1972.

Cunningham, William. *The Growth of English Industry and Commerce.* Cambridge: Cambridge University Press, 1910.

Dickens, Roy S., Jr. *Cherokee Prehistory.* Knoxville: The University of Tennessee Press, 1976.

Durrance, Jill, and William Shamblin, eds. *Appalachian Ways.* Washington, D.C.: Appalachian Regional Commission, 1976.

Dykeman, Wilma. *The French Broad.* Knoxville: The University of Tennessee Press, 1965.

Earle, Alice Morse. *Home Life in Colonial Days.* New York: Macmillan, 1898.

Farrow, John. *Pageant of the Popes.* New York: Sheed & Ward, 1950.

Gazaway, Rena. *The Longest Mile.* New York: Doubleday & Co., 1969: rpt. Baltimore: Penquin Books, 1974.

Green, J. R. *A Short History of the English People.* London: Macmillan & Co., 1917.

Gutman, Judity Mara, *Lewis W. Hine.* New York: Walker & Co., 1967.

Harrison, William. *Elizabethan England.* London: Camelot Classics, 1886.

Kephart, Horace. *Our Southern Highlanders.* Knoxville: The University of Tennessee Press, 1976.

Leach, A. F. *English Schools at the Reformation.* London: Constable, 1896.

——————. *The Schools of Medieval England.* London: Metheun, 1915.

Lewis, M. N., and Madeline Kneberg. *Tribes That Slumber.* Knoxville: The University of Tennessee Press, 1958.

Malone, Harry T. *Cherokees of the Old South: A People in Transition.* Athens: University of Georgia Press, 1956.

Marius, Richard. *Bound for the Promised Land.* New York: Knopf, 1976.

Mason, Robert Lindsay. *The Lure of the Great Smokies.* New York: Houghton Mifflin Co., 1927.

National Geographic Society, ed. *American Mountain People.* Washington, D.C.: n.d.

Nicholls, George. *A History of the English Poor Law.* P. S. King, 1884.

Ogburn, Charlton. *The Southern Appalachians: A Wilderness Quest.* William Morrow & Co., 1975.

Raulston, J. Leonard, and James Livingood. Sequatchie: *A Story of the Southern Cumberlands.* Knoxville: The University of Tennessee Press, 1974.

Rothrock, Mary U., ed. *The French Broad-Holston*

Country. East Tennessee Historical Society, 1946.

Strayer, James R. and Dana C. Munro. *The Middle Ages.* New York: Appleton-Century-Crofts, 1959.

Stone, Gilbert. *A History of Labour.* London: G. G. Harrap & Co., 1921.

Thalmeimer, M. E. *The New Eclectic History of the United States.* New York: American Book Co., 1881.

Thompson, Waddy. *A History of the United States.* New York: Heath, 1904.

Tunis, Edwin. *Colonial Living.* New York: World Publishing Co., 1957.

_____. *Frontier Living.* New York: Thomas Y. Crowell Co., 1961.

_____. *The Young United States.* New York: Thomas Y. Crowell Co., 1969.

Usser, A. P. *An Introduction to the Industrial History of England.* London: G. G. Harrap & Co., 1920.

Weatherford, W. D., and Earl D. C. Brewer. *Life and Religion in Southern Appalachia.* New York: Friendship Press, 1962.

Appendixes

APPENDIX A

*Comparison of Population, Labor Supply and Require-
ments, and Social Conditions in England and Western
Europe with English Colonialism in America in the
Early 1700s.*

In the early 1700s, there was a wide divergence
between population, labor supply, and labor requirements in England and western Europe and the English
Colonies in America. Whereas there were great
economic and social maladjustments in Europe; as
evidenced by massive dislocations resulting in large
numbers of wandering, idle, and starving people
who infested the highways and flocked to the cities;
the English colonies of the New World badly needed
settlers, particularly, to validate their grants of land,
build up the population, supply Europeans with the
commodities they demanded, and raise the colonial
planter from subsistence to prosperity by commanding
the labors of others beside himself.

There was a highly complex pattern of forces producing emigration to the American colonies, but clearly the most powerful force in causing the movement of laboring people was the pecuniary profit to be made by dealing in indentured servitude, redemptioners, and the likes. Labor was one of the few European importations which even the earliest colonists would sacrifice much to procure, and the system of indentured servitude was the most convenient method, next to slavery, by which labor became a commodity to be bought and sold. It was profitable for English merchants trading in the colonies to load their outgoing ships with a cargo of servants, for the labor of those servants could be sold at a price well above transportation costs to colonial planters who needed the labor. Hence, a powerful and resourceful group of merchants and shippers stimulated the emigration and took advantage of the situation to take people to the New World, mostly as servants. What was more important, those merchants and shippers brought pressure to bear on doubtful candidates by advertising the attractions of life in America, and as a last resort they even would collect a shipment of labor by forceful means.[1]

It was in the Virginia Company, probably before 1600, that the customs, habits, and laws of indentured

[1] Abbot Emerson Smith, *Colonists in Bondage* (Gloucester, Mass.: Peter Smith, 1965), p. 5.

servitude were established, they retained essentially the same form throughout cononial history. The ancient institution of apprenticeship was well known, and the fact that a man should sometimes choose, or at other times be forced, to become a bondservant by contract was an acceptable custom. Its application to colonial requirements, however, went through various forms of contracts embodying different terms of agreement, and later the practice of selling servants became quite common. In its early forms and schemes the transported workers and laborers were promised a share of profits and a division of lands for them and their heirs forevermore, after having been transported, lived at the expense of, and labored for the colony for seven years. Deferred rewards, the feeling of servitude rather than partnership, and especially the fact that laborers soon learned that, when the time of dividing came, there was nothing to divide all caused that system to fail.

Then in the early 1600s some laborers, in return for transportation, contracted to work for the Virginia Company one month each year, but they were forced to buy all supplies through the Company and sell all commodities through it. Other schemes saw the Company bringing over laborers and renting them out as servants. A try at abolishing servitude was inaugurated in 1618, when each settler was given an amount of land on which he paid rent to the Company. From time to time the city of London raised funds to take hundreds of children off the streets and transport them to America where they were distributed among free colonists as apprentices. By 1619 groups of young English women were being obtained by the Company and sent to Virginia to become wives of planters. The Company was paid one hundred twenty pounds of tobacco a piece for these women who were to be guarded carefully, not married against their wishes, and forbidden to fall in love with a servant or apprentice.

In 1620 the Virginia Company in London announced its plans for sending to the colony one hundred servants to be disposed of among such planters as offered to defray their charges. Without doubt, there were previous similar cases, but first clearcut instances where colonists paid lump sums to an importer, thereby acquiring full rights and title to the immigrants. As early as 1617 the Virginia Company offered certain merchants and shippers the right to transport settlers to the colony, and by the early 1620s these private merchants and shippers were handling all the transportation and reaping all the profits. By 1624 the customs of indentured servitude had become rather fixed, and the idea of indenturing them in England, Ireland, Scotland, et cetera; and feeding, clothing, and bringing them to America where they would be sold for money or tobacco had become so familiar that the servant traders were ready to bring them in great numbers.

The New England settlements, scanty in agriculture and hostile to newcomers, received few of these servants. However in the Virginia and Maryland colonies, and those further southward, such immigrants were hailed with delight. In the final analysis, most historians agree, more than half of all the immigrants to the colonies south of New England were servants. Thus the principal labor supply until about the mid-eithteenth century was formed as the good, bad, and indifferent poured in, and it was not until the latter part of the eighteenth century that they were supplanted in this respect by Negro slaves. Not until the nineteenth century did an influx of free workers wholly reverse the need for indentured labor.

The usual form of indenture was simple (see Appendix B). It was simply a legal contract whereby a man or woman servant bound himself herself to serve a master in such employments as the master might deem suitable for a given length of time; sometimes the place of indenture was spelled out. In return the master obligated himself to transport food, clothing, drink, and shelter during his service; and perhaps give him some specified reward at the termination of that service, according to the bargain struck by the two persons concerned. Skilled workmen were sometimes entitled to an annual wage and usually were not subject to work as common laborers in the fields. A child's indenture might specify that he be given the rudiments of an education or taught a trade, while German servants often required that they be taught to read the Bible in English. Usually, the length of service varied from four to seven years, but longer terms often were called for in the case of children. There was some diversity in freedom dues (see Appendix C), service indentures variously stipulated clothes, tools, money, or land; generally, however, matters were regulated from early times by custom. Most indentured servants depended upon custom to direct their lives, and their indentures following a common form (see Appendix B for a representative indenture contract of the time).

Generally, each servant carried his indenture contract with him and a copy was furnished the master. While he could be sold only within terms of the contract, this was not always protection against an unjust master. The contract was proof of the length of service required and of freedom dues, if such were special above and beyond customs of the time and place. Servants were strongly advised to make legal and binding contracts, properly signed and sealed, before leaving England, thus reducing disappointments after arrival in the New World. After 1682 English regulation became so strict that such signed and sealed contracts were necessary to protect ships' captains from charges of kidnapping; yet some servants went without written indentures, and others depended only upon oral agreements with merchants, who shipped them, neither groups realizing that both the absence of any agreement as well as merely oral agreement left a servant to the mercy of the system. That practice ultimately caused the evolution of standards known as "customs of the country."

After the Virginia Company had turned over the bringing of servants to privateers, few planters journeyed to England to procure their own servants. Therefore, servants were practically always indentured to a merchant, an immigrant agent, or a ships' captain, and transported like any other cargo. Upon arrival in America the servants were displayed on deck, planters came to inspect them, and their services were sold to the highest bidder. If a servant had an indenture contract in his possession, a note of conditons, price and date was made on its reverse side; thus servant immigration was handled as a business transaction. As mentioned previously, traffic in servants was a very important part of colonial trade, and the populating of English America proceeded according to the most primative law of supply and demand. Throughout the colonial period great numbers of ordinary indentured servants were thus transported legally, while convicts, rogues, vagabonds, political prisoners, and the kidnapped were all taken to colonies as merchandise to be sold as servants (see Appendix D).

Actually, during the seventeenth century indentured servitude was practically the only method by which a poor person could get to the colonies, or by which the planters could obtain white labor. Beginning about the eighteenth century, however, a new scheme appeared as the "redemptioner" took his place alongside the "servant." This was largely the result of increased German and Swiss emigration, which swelled to huge numbers by 1708-9. Large numbers of families left their homes only to arrive at seaports with insufficient funds to finance the remainder of the trip. Accordingly, merchants began to take whatever remaining money the emigrant possessed, putting his family and his goods aboard their ships, and contracting to deliver them to America. Upon arrival the immigrant was allowed a certain period of time (usually fourteen days) to find the balance due the shipper, since it was hoped that he could locate friends to advance the money. However, if the necessary amount could not be raised within the time limit, the immigrant was sold into servitude by the ship's captain for an amount sufficient to satisfy the indebtedness.

Naturally, the redemptionist system generally applied to people who emigrated with families, bringing their goods and chattels with them. Nevertheless, when the redemptionist became a servant, he was in every sense an indentured servant, with no distinctions. As a rule, however, a thoughtful indentured servant who made his contract before departing Europe was free to secure for himself as favorable terms as possible, whereas the redemptionist, executing his indenture of servitude after reaching the colonies, often was forced to accept whatever price and terms were offered. It must be noted, however, that frequently one member of a family would assume the burden of indenture for all the rest.

At the risk of overgeneralization, one might say that indentured servants usually came as cargos of mer-

chandise representing a supply of labor, while redemptioners essentially came as emigrants hopeful
of transplanting themselves to a new home in America.
This observation clarifies the reasons why the redemptionist system flourished in the eighteenth century,
after the colonies had achieved a stable existence
inviting to newcomers, whereas indentured servants;
played a proportionally greater part during the perilous
years of the colonial period

It goes without saying that during colonial times,
although capital was scarce as an element of production, labor was even scarcer. There was no surplus
population during the colonial period and for a century
thereafter, and the only possible recourse was to
Europe. Since no one had sufficient capital to transport large numbers of workers for his own use, the
practice of indentured servitude enabled the colonial
farmer or tradesman to purchase amounts of white
labor just as he would purchase small amounts of any
other European commodity such as clothing or tools.
The migration of indentured servants and redemptioners satisfied that normal economic demand. As a
matter of fact, free white labor became increasingly
procurabel as the colonies grew older, but compared
with indentured labor it was extremly expensive and
very undependable, since it often was not available
when the planter needed it. Where pay in England
for an unskilled worker was about a shilling a day,
the same worker could obtain two, or even perhaps
three, shillings in America, and some artisans and

craftsmen could earn as much as eight shillings six-pence per day. Therefore, a planter who could board a ship near his plantation and buy the services of a carpenter or mason for four years or more was most happy to pay twenty or thirty pounds; even the most unlikely immigrant would probably be worth eight or ten pounds as an indentured servant.

Although it is difficult to understand today, historians say it was the fact that this country offered excellent opportunities for a person eventually to obtain independence that made workers willing to exchange years of their lives for that promised independence, even though they were faced with being purchased for a small capital sum, fed and clothed as cheaply as possible, and kept at their places of work by force if need be. All the facilities and services of colonial law were at the service of masters whose servants ran away, and it was common to see advertisements on billboards and in newspapers offering rewards for recapture of runaways.

Negro slaves, held in perpetual, instead of temporary, servitude answered many colonial requirements, but they did not do away with the economic demand for white servants. Later, Negro slaves became commonly associated with the cotton states or South Carolina, and Georgia, as well as other southern states, but in the Middle Colonies, especially where large amounts of tobacco were grown, the labor of indentured servants was preferred.

During most of the colonial period, a privateer would charge five or six pounds sterling to transport a servant to the New World. That charge, however, represented a figure upon which a merchant could make a profit on his investment; therefore, the actual cost must have been somewhat less than five pounds sterling. Since the cost of transporting a servant usually included food and drink, clothing, and expenses while awaiting departure from Europe, naturally the amount varied greatly. For example, there are recorded cases in which the cost of procuring a servant in Europe, equipping, and getting him to the colonies was as much as ten pounds; however, the price was generally less. Thus, indentured servants delivered to the colonies might cost the planter eleven or twelve pounds apiece, but if a merchant or shipowner brought them through his own initiative and with his own investment, he would sell them for whatever the current demand of labor dictated. Sometimes, therefore, an indentured laborer would sell for as little as twelve pounds, and while sometimes a craftsman or artisan might bring as much as sixty pounds. Generally, however, a merchant who spent four to ten pounds to ship a servant to America could count on selling him for somehere between six and thirty pounds. The price was much more unstable for a child, who generally brought from one to five pounds Scottish servants were deemed the best, for the most part, and Irish Catholics the worst.

Clearly, the servant himself was highly exploited in the transaction, for he was sold for a much higher figure than the cost of his passage. If he could have obtained the requisite five pounds, he might have paid his own passage and then, if he desired, sold himself into servitude, keeping any profit for himself. Very few, however, could raise such an amount, and of those who could, still fewer wanted to spend it on emigrating; in fact, real stimulus to emigration at that time was not the desire of servants to go to America but rather the desire of merchants to secure them as a cargo.

A great many of our contemporaries are prone to believe that, since a large proportion of Europeans were poor, discouraged, and exploited at home, the mere fact that there was chance for improvement elsewhere, and those poor wretches learned of that chance, satisfactorily explained the emigration that took place. That is far from the truth. The fact is most people have been poor and exploited, thoughout history, but phenomena alone rarely provided justification for any emigration that took place. On the contrary, only goaded by the most extreme difficulty, no matter how miserable the conditions at home, have masses of people been persuaded to cut loose from their ancient ties and try a new country. Nevertheless, although poverty and discontent are not necessarily causes of emigration, they are characteristic of the people who take part in it.

It is easy to document the fact that a majority

of the English population was poor: Gregory estimated in 1688 that, for more than half the English population, the annual expenses were greater than the annual income, with the differences being made up by the poor rates.* Nor was the existence of poverty remarkable or unknown in any age. The important fact is that poverty, as it existed in England in the early 1700s, was a symptom of the unstable society. That is, it was not rooted in the old and permanent order of things, but rather most of it resulted from the transition from a feudal to a commercial economy, and subsequently from a commercial to an industrial economy. Many thousands of already poor were dislodged from ancestral homes and occupations and turned out to wander the highways. Thus came into existence masses of poor people characterized by their mobility and lack of attachment to any place or occupation. They streamed into towns and cities in such numbers that lawmakers were alarmed and convinced that the country was overpopulated. London and other large cities grew with such rapidity that even the most stringent laws of vagrancy could not be enforced. There was a cry to relieve the land of its surplus inhabitants, and thus the climate and opinion were set toward emigration.

Mass migration due to religious discontent appeared among the Puritans in the 1630s. Nearly a century later Ireland showed some symptoms of mass emigration, as did Scotland and Germany in the 1770s. By and large, however, those few instances of mass migration comprised only a miniscule portion of those who emigrated as indentured servants.

The latter were secured as cargo by means of pamphlets, speeches—other more drastic measures—all designed to convince them that they would be exercising sound judgement in escaping from the economic, political, and religious maladjustments of the bad old world to the golden opportunities of the new. Most contemporary writers, however, charged that emigrants were all sadly deceived and imposed upon by false propaganda and lying agents; if they had known what they were doing, they would have stayed at home. It is well known that the methods of securing a cargo ranged from those which were legal and aboveboard to others which were surreptitious and disreputable, extending even to forcible kidnapping. Often it was very difficult to fix the point at which legitimate means of recruiting blended into the illegitimate.

There are many records of a merchant or tradesman who decided to freight a ship legitimately with servants and send it to the American plantations. For example, when one J. Abernathy was employed to recruit and manage a cargo, it took him from the first of January to the middle of May, when the ship sailed to secure the cargo. He hired drummers to go through the town of Aberdeen, Scotland, announcing the voyage, and he sent pipers to fairs and out amongst the people for the same purpose. As prospective servants came in, he bound them legally before a migistrate; even gave a gold watch and chain here and there, and gave tobacco to all; furthermore, he boarded and lodged them and was careful to keep them content with beautiful stories of the bountiful life in the colonies.

Thus, large numbers of servants were recruited for a particular enterprise, but still larger numbers were collected by free-lance agents who were not connected with any particular voyage, but rather were permanently in the trade as collector of sevant candidates. Generally, public opinion was hostile to them because many of the more knowledgeable people believed that a great part of the gents' success was due to misrepresentation, fraud, and secrecy.

Added to the fact that public opinion was generally unfavorable to servant recruiters was the general feeling prevalent in the early 1700s among factory owners and managers that the labor supply of Great Britain was rapidly being depleted to an unacceptable level. Therefore, those factory owners and managers mounted a campaign to Parliament to discourage emigration so that Britain could keep the working class as their own labor supply for their own factories. Thus the tug-of-war continued between the colonists who needed labor and the English factory owners and managers who wanted to keep the best labor supply at home.

Nevertheless, as the plantations in the colonies developed and the demand for servants increased, a situation was created which offered too great a temptation to the greed of many persons in England. Vessels were constantly leaving for the colonies, and the owners and captains, eager to acquire a load of serv-

ants, would pay a few pounds for each candidate produced and ask no questions. There were plenty of un-
savory characters around London and other seaport
towns who would not hesitate to collect a few wandering children, simpleminded adults, or even drunkards
asleep in the gutter, and sell them to a shipmaster.
Once aboard ship, the unfortunate victims never saw
the light of day until the ship was at sea. This practice
merged into what is commonly known as "the next
step," and that was the use of *spirits* on the idle, lazy,
and simple—or those who would rather beg than
work—and after having imbibed the liquors the prospective servant would take courage and agree to be
transported. If the drink did not work, that is, if the
victim did not become sodden and manageable, he
might even be kidnapped. Children were often enticed
by presents or sweets, then concealed in secure haunts
until they could be shipped. It is most likely that from
those times and practices the term "being spirited
away" was coined.

The practices of spiriting soon began to frighten
the lower classes of Londoners, and the English government began to move to check the practice by the late
1630s and early 1640s. However, in spite of searching
ships for such children, forcing a registry of all outgoing passengers to the colonies or any foreign parts,
and the receipts of certificates of arrival by the governor of each province, it is said that the spiriting and
kidnapping of servants went on with increasing vigor.
It must be remembered, too, that the spiriters and

kidnappers were not only man-stealers but were also the hope and refuge of thousands of persons who wished to flee the country for various reasons.

There were other categories of people sold into indentured servitude, but in describing them I will be very brief indeed. There was (1) convict transportation prior to 1718, (2) convict transportation after 1718, (3) transportation of rogues and vagabonds, and (4) political and military prisoners. I will devote one paragraph to each of these categories, not in the hope of doing justice to the subject matter, but merely to give the reader some idea of the scope and source of indentured servitude in the early American colonies.

Convict transportation prior to 1718 was relatively scarce. It has been previously noted that as the agricultural economy of England became a mercantile economy, a tremendous gap widened between the rich and the poor, with a resulting increase in thieves, robbers, and other criminals. As thousands were turned away from their ancestral manorial occupations, they were set adrift and subsequently swarmed to the cities as idle, masterless, unwanted persons who lived by whatever devices they could invent. Inevitably they stole and robbed and thus became a blight on society. In the seventeenth century Parliament designated some three hundred crimes as felonies—and the death penalty was prescribed by law for all felonies. Felonies included housebreaking or stealing anything of value greater than a shilling; thus thousands of persons guilty of negligible crimes were sentenced to the gallows. The pleadings of clergy freed many convicts if they could read, but the royal pardon was of most significance because it often gave a reprieve to "worthy" felons who would transport themselves out of the country. King James I instituted that practice as early as 1614, when he gave some of his nobles and justices power to reprieve felons for any specific foreign undertaking and for any fixed length of time. At first that law was used sparingly, but it is recorded that between 1661 and 1700 about five thousand convicts were thus destined for the colonies. A seven-year exile was common for those thus chosen or pardoned. Actual shipment was performed by merchants trading in the colonies, and conditions of the pardon usually charged the sheriff with making arrangements with merchants (sometimes even a specific merchant), who made their profit by selling the convicts as indentured servants in the colonies. It is not absolutely clear who decided which felon would be reprieved, but the author suspects the transfer of money was a prime factor, especially, since records show that a jailer's fee might be forty shillings, but a "preparation house" for the shipment of convicts might be willing to pay as high as three pounds. Who participated in these divisions of money is not clear, in the sources which the author checked. It must be mentioned, however, that many convicts not deemed suitable for plantation labor were used in the military forces.

With the ending of the French wars and disbandment of armies after 1713, the problem of what to do with the hordes of convicted felons became even more serious. In 1717 Parliament passed a law stating that any felon "within the benefit of clergy" would be banished for seven years; persons convicted of non-clergyable felonies for which death was the penalty but whom the king pardoned for transportation should be handed over to a contractor for fourteen years. The law provided that premature return from that transportation should be handed over to a contractor for fourteen years. The law provided that premature return from that transportation was cause for death, and it simplified the machinery of waiting for pardons to be made out and sealed. Agreements were made with merchants who were subsidized for transporting the prisoners; in return, they guaranteed to receive and transport all felons regardless of age, lameness, and infirmity, to pay jailers and all other transportation fees, and to guarantee prisoners' nonreturn to England "through any fault of the merchant." Various merchants secured these subsidized contracts, which paid several pounds for each convict transported, but by 1772 the market for servants in the American colonies was so good that several merchants were willing to do it for nothing. Thus, between 1719 and 1772, three contractors alone took 17,740 felons from the Home Counties—those adjacent to London—and from Newgate Prison, put them aboard ship, and started them for the colonies. One writer asserts that Great Britain bestowed upon America a total of 30,000 felons during the eighteenth century.[2]   Although some cannot be traced, most convicts went to Maryland and Virginia. Some colonies refused convicts altogether, some levied fines on their entry, but by and large, the profits made by the contractors were good. English opinion held that the transportation of criminals to the American colonies was a good and humane thing, but the opinion of both colonists and convicts was not the same. Some convicts even said that they would have preferred hanging to the suffering they had undergone. Some colonists claimed that crime rates skyrocketed and that they were in fact political penal colonies. The latter grievance was untrue, since the unsegregated felons were blended into the civil population. Actually, resentment against the English government was considered exaggerated, because the truth is that felons were received with open arms in greater and greater numbers by planters who wanted cheap labor.

An Elizabethan statue of about 1560 contains a famous passage in which Parliament defined rogues and vagabonds (see Appendix D); that definition remained English law for more than two centuries. Such person, when found, were stripped and whipped until bloody, then sent either to their birthplaces or present places of residence; if neither of these places should be available to them, they were sent to prison unless someone would offer them employment. Any justice who chose could banish them as felons even

[2]Smith, *op. cit.*, p. 117.

before the law of 1717. Thus many rogues and vagabonds were sent to the colonies under the 1614 law of
King James I, some were resettled in England, and
some spent a lifetime in prison. A great number of
that horde of humanity were children under twelve.
After the 1660s it was decreed that "sturdy beggars fit
to be transported, nor incorrigibles, who will go to
English plantations," would be excepted from the
common punishment of whipping and resettling, and
would be disposed of in the usual way of indentured
servants for a term not exceeding seven years. Thus,
large numbers of potential indentured servants fell
into the hands of private merchants who eventually
sold them in the American colonies. Thousands of
poor English children were sent to Virginia, while
under similar acts Portugal sent many children to the
East Indies. For some of those English children passage was paid by charitable organizations or individuals, but for the most part the Virginia Company paid
the passage, gave five pounds for expenses, and apprenticed the children until they were twenty-one
years of age. In the year 1627 alone, fourteen or fifteen
hundred children were gathered from many places in
Great Britain and sent to Virginia. It was not at all
unusual for part of the cargo to be kidnappers, if such
were needed to finish out a cargo, and there were
many occasions when it was necessary to search vessels
for kidnapped persons.[3]

[3] Smith, *op. cit.*, p. 146

Just prior to 1649, when both Charles I's reign and the Civil war were drawing to an end, the supremacy of Cromwell's armies were unquestioned, and at each encounter many prisoners were taken, the majority of which were Scottish. Since these prisoners could neither be detained in England nor sent home with full safety to the parliamentary cause, as their numbers swelled it became necessary to send them into exile. Some were sold as mercenary soldiers, some were sent to Ireland, but most were sent to plantations in the American colonies, with merchants being invited to contract for such shipment. Merchants offering the best security and guarantee that such prisoners would not return to England were given first choice. Few actual records of the many shiploads thus sent out of England exist today.

Whereas, in dealing with the English and Scots it was rather easy to separate shipments of political and military prisoners from the regular dealings in rogues, vagabonds, and felons, as for the Irish it was practically impossible to make that distinction. Although by far the largest number of Irish were transported to American colonial plantations as rogues and vagabonds, the reasons for their thus being classified were in themselves political—that is their wretched conditions resulted directly from their rebellions against Irishmen ended up in the great melting pot of indentured servitude in the American colonies.

APPENDIX B

A Sample Indenture Contract

This Indenture made the 21st day of February 1682/3 Between Rich. Browne age 33 years of the one party, and Francis Richardson of the other party, witnesseth, that the said Richard Browne doth thereby covenant, promise, and grant to & with the said Francis Richardson his Executors & Assigns, from the day of the date hereof, until his first & next arrival at New York or New Jersey and after, for and during the term of foure years, to serve in such service & imployment, as he the said Francis Richardson or his Assigns shall there imploy him according to the custom of the country in the like kind - In consideration whereof, the said Francis Richardson doth hereby covenant and grant to and with the said Richard Browne to pay for his passing, and to find and allow him meat, drink, apparrell, and lodging, with other necessaries, during the said term, & at the end of the said term to pay him according to the Custom of the Country

In Witness thereof the parties above mentioned to these indentures have interchangeably set their Hands and Seals the day and year written above.

Source: Abbot Emerson Smith, *Colonists in Bondage* (Gloucester, Mass.: Peter Smith, 1965), p. 18.

APPENDIX C

Freedom Dues according to Customs of the Country

Barbados
    1647 - Land in Nevis or Antiqua (Proclamation by the Earl of Carlisle; not of permanent effect).

    1661 - 400 lbs. muscovado sugar.

Nevis
    1672 - 10 pounds Sterling ''according to former custom.''
    1675 - 800 lbs of sugar.
    1681 - 400 lbs. of sugar.
    1701 - 400 lbs of sugar, or fifty shillings.

Antiqua
    1669 - 400 lbs of sugar or tobacco.

St. Christopher

> 1722 - Four pounds of current money or 600 lbs. of sugar.

Jamaica

> 1661/2 - 30 acres of land (Instructions ot Governor Lord Windor).
>
> 1661 - 400 lbs. of sugar (order of council).
>
> 1664 - Forty shillings or 40 acres of land.
>
> 1681 - Forty shillings.

South Carolina

> (During the proprietary period, various amounts of land were promised and alloted).
>
> 1717 - One new hat, a good coat and breeches either of kersey or broadcloth, one new shirt of white linen, one new pair of shoes and stockings. For women servants: a "Wast coat and Petticoat of new Half-thicks or Pennistone, a new shift of white Linnen; a new pair of shoes and stockings, a blue Apron or two Caps of white Linnen." (Continued in Act of 1744.)
>
> 1730 - The crown offers fifty acres of land, free of quitrent for ten years.

North Carolina

> (During the proprietary period, land was given, e.g. in 1686, 50 acres at one penny quitrent).
>
> 1715 - Three barrels of Indian corn and two new

APPENDIX C • 245

suits of a value of at least 5 pounds Sterling.

1741 - Three pounds proclamation money and one sufficient suit.

Virginia

1705 - 10 bushels of corn, 30 shillings or the equivalent, One musket worth at least 20 shillings. To women servants: 15 bushels of corn and forty shillings.

1748 - Three pounds 10 shillings of current money.

1753 - The same.

Maryland

1640 - One good Cloth suite of Keirsey or broad cloth, A shift of white linen, one new pair stockings and shoes two hoes one axe 3 barrells of Corne and 50 acres of land— Women servants: a years provision of Corne and a like proportion of Cloths and land.

1699 the corn is ommitted and instead is given a hat and a gun. Continued in 1715. (Land was not given after 1683).

Pennsylvania

Penn promised 50 acres of land during the first years.

1682 - One new suit, 10 bushels of wheat or 14 of corn, one axe, two hoes.

1700 - Two complete suits of clothes, one of which is to be new; one new axe, one grubbing hoe and one weeding hoe.

1771 - The same, but minus two hoes.

New Jersey

1682 - seven bushels of corn, two suits of clothes, two hoes and an axe. (Also land).

New York

No law fixing freedom dues, except of Duke of York's Laws identical for those for Massachusetts.

Massachusetts

1641 - Servants must not be sent away empty.

Source: Abbot Emerson Smith, *Colonists in Bondage* (Gloucester, Mass.: Peter Smith, 1965), pp. 238-40.

APPENDIX D

Rogues and Vagabonds

All persons calling themselves Schollers going about, all Seafaring men pretending losses of their Shippes or goods on the sea going about the Country begging, all idle persons going about in any Country eyther begging or using any subtile Crafte or unlawful Games or Playes, or fayning themselves to have knowledge in Phisiognomye Palmestry or other like crafty Scyence, or pretending that they can tell Destenyes Fortunes or such other like fantasticall Imagynacons; all persons that be or utter themselves to be Proctors Procurers Patent Gatherers or Collectors for Gaoles Prisons or Hospitals; all Fencers Bearwards comon Players of Enterludes and Minstrells wandering abrode (other than Players of Interludes belonging to any Baron of the Realme . . .); all juglers Tynkers Pedlars and Petty Chapmen wandring abrode; all wandring persons and common Labourers being persons able in Bodye using loytering, and refusing to worcke for such reasonable wages as is taxed or comonly given in such parts where such persons do or shall happen dwell or abide; not having otherwyse to maynteyne themselves; all persons delivered out of Gaoles that begg for their Fees, or otherwise do travayle begging; all such persons shall wander abroade begging pretending losses by Fyre or otherwise; and all such persons not being Fellons wandring and pretending themselves to be Egipcyans, or wandring in the Habite or Attrye of counterfayte Egipcians.

Source: Abbot Emerson Smith, *Colonists in Bondage* (Gloucester, Mass.: Peter Smith, 1965), pp. 136-37.

Jamie's Journey Westward

I have retraced Jamie's journey from the Savedge, as he fled westward, and the route he took was west by very slightly south. He skirted Petersburg to the south, crossed Stony Creek and Nottaway River, and passed by Fort Pickett to the south, through what is now the town of Alberta. He crossed the upper forks of the Meherrin River; the large river which he encountered the fourth day was the Staunton. His route took him through what is now South Boston and north of Danville, for the six creeks he crossed on the eleventh day are just northwest of what is now Danville. The summit where he spent the night and reoriented himself was Aiken Summit. From there the mountain for which he aimed was Pilot Mountain, which rises three thousand feet in elevation. The tall mountain which he could see to the northwest was Mount Airy; Stone Mountain and Ski Mountain were among the ridges and smaller mountains visible; the Great Smoky

Mountains loomed beyond in the blue haze. As he headed into the foothills of the Great Smokies, he crossed the Aratat and Fischer rivers and become entangled and confused in the various branches of the Yadkin River, before crossing more mountain ranges to find the south fork of the New River. In his confusion and lethargy he wandered down the New River until he discovered he confluence of the south and north forks, when he headed west again. During his journey up the north fork of the New River he encountered the Indians. His further journey to the valley of the Pellissippi can be followed easily on a map.

APPENDIX F

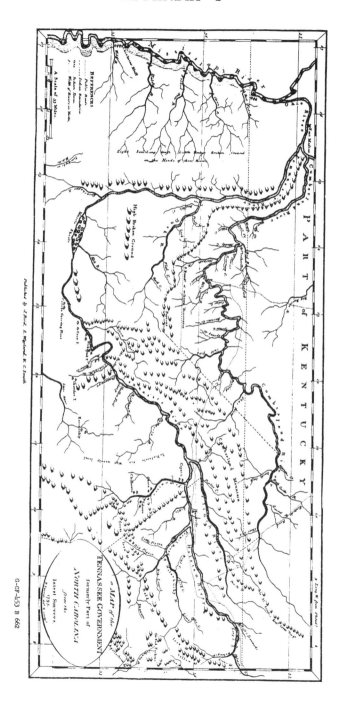

Early Map with Original Indian Names of Rivers

APPENDIX   H

Natural Barriers

Somewhere around the end of the 17th Century the well-known Cherokee nation began to extend its settlements into eastern Tennessee from the southern end of the Appalachian mountain region.   At this period the southeastern native tribes had been encroached on by white men from the direction of the east coast for some 170 years. The Appalachian mountains had been an effective barrier to white penetrations, but south of the mountains the pressure of the Europeans was much greater, with the result that many of the more southern Indian nations seemed to have withdrawn their settlements from the peripheries and to have become more compactly settled in the interior regions of Georgia and Alabama. As the Indian tribes who had formerly made their homes along the eastern seaboard and in the piedmont region of the Carolinas and Virginia were forced to give way before the European invasion, they created a pressure upon the interior tribes, such as the Cherokee, in the mountain valleys. Coincident with the withdrawal of the Muskhogean tribes, who were represented in the valley of eastern Tennessee by the Dallas people, the Cherokee began to push their settlements down the Little Tennessee River valley. They gradually extended their control over the broad territories which they later claimed in their negotiations with the colonial and United States governments.

There is sufficient evidence in writings of the 18th Century to indicate that the Cherokee and the various Muskhogean tribes engaged in local conflicts as a result of this displacement of peoples, but there is no evidence that there was any widespread conquest by the Cherokee. The 18th Century was a period of conflict and accommodation between the strong Indian nations themselves on one hand, and between the Indian and white man on the other. Perhaps one should add that at the same time a third type of struggle was also going on between the various nations of white men with colonial aspirations. This latter conflict complicated relationships between the Indian groups still further since the Europeans took advantage of native rivalries and sought allies amongst the Indians who would best advance their own aims.

Archaeological evidence points to the apparent fact that the Cherokee were long established at the southern end of the Appalachian range. Because their language is related to that of the Iroquois, students have inferred that the Cherokee were an offshoot of the Iroquois who had moved southward to take up their abode in the Appalachian mountain valley. Our recent unfinished studies, however, indicate that the reverse may have taken place, namely, that the Iroquois split off from the Cherokee and moved to the Northeast. This deduction is derived largely from studies of pottery obtained from ancient archaeological sites in Georgia and later Cherokee sites in North Carolina and Tennessee. The surface designs on the pottery vessels resemble those employed by the Cherokee in later prehistoric times and during the early historic period. Hence, there are scientific grounds for the assumption that the ancient Georgia sites were occupied by the ancestral Cherokee. Inasmuch as the latter sites extend back to possible 1000 A.D. or earlier, and since the Iroquois are not thought to have established themselves in the Northeast at so early a date, the implications are that the Cherokee are a portion of the original group which remained behind when the northeasterly migration occured. Furthermore, the Cherokee language seems to be an older form of the Iroquois, which again suggests a southeastern origin for the Iroquois.

There is little that can be said at present regarding the prehistoric customs of the Cherokee, due to deficient archaeological data. Early narrators, such as Bartram and Adair, have left a rather confused picture. These early observers were unskilled in ethnological methods and were prone to give general descriptions of the southeastern tribes, rather than specific descriptions of individual tribes. The first contacts of the

Cherokee with the white man were with the intrepid Scotch traders who made their way across the mountains and established themselves in the main Cherokee villages where they frequently married prominent women of the tribe. Generally these traders were men of integrity and were respected by the Cherokee and colonial governments of Virginia and Carolina.

Source: Mary U. Rothrock, ed., *Frence Broad-Holston Country* (Knoxville: East Tennessee Historical Society, 1946), pp. 9-11.

APPENDIX I

The Melungeons

In these few pages the author presents his theory concerning the origin of the *Melungeons*. It is based on historical research, interviews with noted anthropoligists, and a personal knowledge of the *Melungeons,* the latter both from having spent the first eighteen years of his life in close geographic proximity to them, and having friends and relatives still living in that geographic area. In actual fact, the author admits, his theory has been. formulated primarily from among the many presented in the "Suggested Readings," in combination with his knowledge of early European history. The author emphasizes, however, that if the reader is to obtain a decent understanding of the *Melungeons,* the five "Suggested Readings" at the end of this Appendix are a minimum requirement.

The first known settlers in Spain, generally believed to have emigrated from North Africa, were Iberians; from them the Iberian Peninsula received its name. After them Celtic-speaking tribes overran a large part of the peninsula and mingled with the Iberians, thus forming the mixed people, very likely olive-skinned, known as Celtiberians. Later, Spain was conquered by Carthaginians, who left few traces of their occupation; by Romans, who thoroughly Romanized the country; by Visigoths, who founded a Germanic kingdom; and lastly by the dark-skinned, mixed Arab and Berber people known as the Moors, who introduced Arabic culture and the faith of Islam.

It is well known that the Moslems, Moors, or Mohammedans descended from Bedouin Arabs who claim Ishmael, the son of Abraham and half brother of Isaac, as their ancestors. It is equally well known, however, that the term "Arab" or "Moor," possibly of more cultural than ethnic significance, in a broad sense describes a collection of dark-skinned tribes who claim, accurately or not, a predominantly caucasian ancestry. [1] Nevertheless, they were, and still are, a dark-skinned people who are recognized as an ethnic grouping.

A second historical fact to remember is that, during those early times, the entire Iberian Peninsula was referred to as "Spain." The Christian state of Portugal arose on the west coast of the peninsula, just as other Christian states such as Leon, Castile, Navarre, and Aragon evolved in the area. Portugal like the rest, belonged to Spain, from which it was separated only by artificial frontiers. In later years Portugal managed

Encyclopaedia Britannica, 1954 ed., vol. 2, p. 198.

to win and maintain independence from Spain, but in general, the Portuguese people could not then, nor now, be distinguished from the Spanish. Therefore, for one to say that the Melungeons descended from the Portuguese rather than the Spanish is a moot point.

Considering the above historical facts and the history of the Middle Ages in general, one can reasonably surmise that the Spanish people, like most western Europeans during the Middle Ages, classified themselves by origin, cultural habits, and the color of their skin; great social distance often existed between the various groups as to class, privilege, and citizenship. Also, those persons of Roman and German heritage—the so-called pure "white Europeans"—considered themselves the elite of society; as the groups of dark-skinned peoples became increasingly and economically deprived. It is well known that by the time of DeSota's explorations and the building of the Spanish Armade the military and social leaders were strictly white caucasian, and the peasants, the working classes, or the able seamen were of darker-skinned Moorish descent. Most historians agree, therefore, that the personnel of the Spanish Armada and the exploratory expeditions was composed of a few white European officers, a slightly darder-skinned group of all, made up the working classes, able seamen, and slaves.

In 1540 Hernando DeSoto's exploratory party of more than seven hundred fifty men, together with over two hundred horses,[2] were searching for gold

[2]*Encyclopaedia Britannica*, 1954 ed., vol. 21, p. 4.

in the New World; they penetrated the interior as far
as the present site of Knoxville at the confluence
of the Hogohegee (Holston) and Cootclas (French
Broad rivers.[3] Many historians agree, that Chief Attakullakulla's legèndary version of DeSoto's encounter
with his ancestors, described on pages 205-6, was
fairly accurate in that DeSoto was far from kind to the
natives but rather attacked and killed many thousands
for no apparent reason. Attakullakulla's story of the
great battle between DeSoto and the Cherokee nation is
considered essentially true, and it is likely that the six
men of DeSoto's expedition who were captured by the
Cherokee belonged to the Moorish, dark-skinned
ethnic group of Spaniards.

In addition, it is reaonable to believe that the
six captured men, during their stay with the Cherokee,
were alert enough to discern the excellent relationship
that existed between the Cherokee and the English
contrasted to the poor one between the Cherokee and
both the French and the Spanish; so, when the six
were set free, given Cherokee wives, and banished to
the upper reaches of the Pellissippi, they knew that
they would have to pretend to be English for their own
protection and well being. There is little doubt that
they began to assume English names and English
ways.

It is the author's theory that the six whom the
Cherokee called *Melungos* and banished, along with

[3]Jean Patterson Bible, *Melungeons Yesterday and Today*
(Rogersville, Tenn.: East Tennessee Printing Company, 1975),
p. 95.

Cherokee wives, to the upper reaches of the Pellissippi in the early 1540s eventually assimilated black runaway slaves, other dark-skinned strangers who came their way, and an occasional white European on the run from the law; thus, over a period of two hundred years, they developed into the strange clan known as the *"Melungeons."* Although, as stated above, it is probable that the six original *Melungos* were smart enough to realize that typical English names would be necessary for their long-term welfare and protection it is just as probable that it was the ''occasionally assimilated white European'' (perhaps even remants of the Roanoke Island Settlement of 1584) who converted the clan's language to English and introduced such typically English family names as Bowling, Brogan, Collins, Mullins, Goins, Gibson, Goodman, Moore, et cetera.[4] The derivation of the word "Melungeon" is interesting. Attakullakulla's ancestors heard DeSota himself refer to a certain group of his men as *Melungos,* an Afro-Portuguese term meaning "shipmate" or "companion".[5] Also, French trappers came into the area of the upper Pellissippi in 1714, and it is believed that they, too, came in contact with the strange clan of people whom they designated *Melungeons,* meaning "mixture" or "of mixed blood."[6] These two terms

[4] All of the suggested readings at the end of this Appendix refer to these same names, among others.

[5] Bible, *op. cit.*, p. 11.

[6] Bonnie Ball, *The Melungeons,* 1969. Self-Published, available in The University of Tennessee Library at Knoxville.

rapidly merged into the white European term *Melungeon*, and because the clan was unusual in that they were *colored* rather than white, the word *Melungeon* referred to a people deemed to be inferior by whites.

In Jamie's time they were very much like Mary in appearance. Their dark skin was olive colored, rather than copper or black; They had straight black hair and eye coloring ranging all the way from black to brown to purple to grey. Their cheek bones were high, like those of the Cherokee, but unlike either the Indian or Negro, they had thin lips and narrow faces. The men were generally tall, agile, alert, industrious, quiet, and scrupulous traders. The young women were strikingly beautiful; in general they bore many of the same characteristics as the men, except that they tended to grow more obese in their later years. Authors of the "Suggested Readings" listed below attest to the fact that as time went on, the term *Melungeon* became an even more derogatory designation, and few would admit to being a *Melungeon*. Ironically, many inhabitants of Hancock County are proud to be called descendants of Melungeons.[7] Yet one can travel throughout Hancock County and the far reaches of the Clinch River Valley and without discerning a true *Melungeon*, for intermarriage and the passage of time have all but wiped out that singularly distinctive group of original settlers.

Permit me to mention one other bit of history which reveals the origin of a peculiar grouping of people

[7]Bible, *op. cit.*, p. 11.

who trace their ancestry back to the sixteenth century. To wit, it is a well-known fact that, when the Spanish Armada was defeated in the English Channel in 1588, a few survivors of the battle and the subsequent wrecks of the Spanish ships made their way to the coasts of Scotland and Ireland, where they escaped capture by going inland, hiding out, and eventually marrying native women. Those intermarriages resulted in a peculiar grouping of people who, even today, refer to themselves as "black Irish" or "black Scotch."

SUGGESTED READINGS

Ball, Bonnie. *The Melungeons.* 1969. Self-Published. Available in The University of Tennessee Library, Knoxville.

Bible, Jean Patterson. *Melungeons Yesterday and Today.* Rogersville, Tenn.: East Tennessee Printing Co., 1975.

Price, Edward T. "The Melungeons: A Mixed-Blood Strain of the Southern Appalachians." *Geographical Review,* No. 2 (Apr. 1951), pp. 256-71.

Price, Henry R. "The Vanishing Colony of Newman's Ridge." A paper presented at the Spring Meeting of the American Studies Association of Kentucky and Tennessee, Tennessee Technological University, Cookeville, Tenn., March 25-26, 1966.

Willis, Thurston L. "The Melungeons of Eastern Tennessee." *The Chesopiean 9 (Feb., Apr., June 1971):2.*

APPENDIX J

Partially Proven Theory of the
Antecedents of John Breeding

(A-1) James & Sarah Breeding
    Children △

(A-2) Jeremiah - Elizabeth Hurst
    (Married 4-29-1788)

(A-3) Bryant - Winney
(A-4) Elizabeth- Aaron Perry
(A-5) Byron

(B-1) Spencer Breeding, Sr (D. before 1808)
    Children

(B-2) Spencer, Jr. - Winifred Hurst △
    (Married 11-24-1789)

(B-3) Elizabeth   - Wharton Nunn
(B-4) Sylvia   - Jacob Cupp
(B-5) Nancy

(AB-1) John Breeding   - - - Married - - - Elizabeth Stone
    B. 1-27-1797   Jan.1826   B. 4-22-1808
    D. 2-21-1871   D. 5-20-1883

△ Daughter of "Mill Creek John Hurst"

△ Daughter of Abasalom Hurst, brother to "Mill Creek John Hurst"

△ This is "New River Spencer" and is not to be confused with "Clinch River
Spencer" of Russell County, Virginia, whose history is aptly covered in
Clarice Breeding's book, The Genealogy of Spencer Breeding. This Spencer
had 18 children by three wives. Several had the same names as "New River
Spencers"- and this could become confusing to persons who don't know the
difference.

Source: The first five pages of this Appendix were furnished by Mr. Earl J.
Breeding, 105 California Avenue, Oak Ridge, Tennessee 37830.
However, the last four pages, i.e. the author's paternal lineage
from Byron Breeding, was drawn from many sources and put together
as such by the author.

A-1 James and Sarah Breeding

James Breeding was originally located in Shenandoah County, Virginia.
From 1783 to 1792, he was listed on the Tax Lists (land tax); then he
disappeared on Shenandoah Tax Lists but appeared as a taxpayer in Wythe
County, Virginia, in 1793, along New River and Little Reed Creek where
the Hursts and Breedings were relocating. Records show him selling 90
acres to Thomas Hurst in 1804. This was the Thomas Hurst who married
Sylvia Breeding, moved to Lee County, Virginia, and then to Claiborne
County, Tennessee, where he was pastor of the Big Springs Primitive
Baptist Church. Sarah's maiden name is unknown to me. It is probable
-nat James and Sarah lived out their lives along New River in Wythe
County, Virginia. I have ño further records.

A-2 Jeremiah Breeding

Jeremiah Breeding from Shenandoah County, Virginia, married Elizabeth
Hurst 4-29-1788 (see <u>Shenandoah County Marriage Bonds 1772-1850</u> by
Bernice Ashby and <u>Hurst of Shenandoah</u> by J. C. Hurst). The former
states that Jeremiah was the son of James Breeding. Jeremiah was on
Shenandoah County, Virginia, Tax Lists from 1790 to 1797. He then
shows up on Wythe County, Virginia, Tax Lists from 1797 to 1800. He
is found in Lee County, Virginia, in 1801, where he bought land from
Stephen Thompson (D.B-1, Page 230). Bryant and Byron Breeding, his
brothers, witnessed this deed as well as Aaron Perry, the husband of
his sister Elizabeth.

A-3 Bryant Breeding

There is no record of Bryant Breeding owning land in Shenandoah County,
Virginia, but he is listed on Tax Lists of Wythe County as early as
1803. In 1811, "Brient" Breeding and his wife "Winney" sold 100 acres
to Spencer Breeding, Jr., on the "east side of New River". I believe
that shortly thereafter he moved to Claiborne County, Tennessee, where
he bought land in the Barren Creek area. Later moving to the Sycamore
Creek area of the county. He is listed as a member of the Big Springs
Primitive Baptist Church* received by letter in Nov., 1819. In May,
1820, Fanny Breeding, Bryant's second wife, was received. Fanny's
maiden name was Harper. Bryant died prior to 1831, the year his will
was probated. There is a branch history being compiled of Bryant's
descendants. There are two tribes of Breedings in Claiborne County
who do not claim or understand their kinship--that of John Breeding,
AB-1, and those of Bryant.

---

* The 3rd oldest Church in Tennessee founded by Rev. Tidence Lane
and others. A small log Church is still standing and in active use by
the Primitive Baptist founded when Tennessee was still a part of North
Carolina.

A-4 Elizabeth Breeding

In the book <u>Shenandoah County Marriage Bonds 1772-1850</u> by Bernice Ashby,
it is stated that Elizabeth is the daughter of James and Sarah Breeding.
I do not have much information on Aaron Perry except that he witnessed a
deed for Jeremiah Breeding in Lee County, Virginia in 1801. Her marriage
to Aaron Perry was July 7, 1789. I assume that the Perrys were moving
along with the Breedings and Hursts.

A-5 Byron Breeding (Byram) (Byrem)
     B. 1772 D. 2-23-1832
The first notice of Byron Breeding that I can find is the witnessing of
the deed of Stephen Thompson to Jeremiah Breeding in Lee County, Virginia
in 1801. At this time he would have been 29 years of age. John, his
first son, would have been 4 years old. Among John Breeding's papers is
a contract signed by Nancy, his mother, and Charity Fugate, who later
married William Breeding of New River. The contract was dated 1819 when
John was 22 years of age.

Byron Breeding purchased 100 acres of land in Lee County,
Virginia in 1803 and in 1805 "Byron Breeding and Jane, his
wife sold the same 100 acres to John Fritts.

On Sept. 3, 1810, "Byrem" Breeding and Jean, his wife, of Roane County,
Tennessee, sold Abasalom Hurst land on the waters of "Little Reed
Island Creek". The deed is signed "Byram". The confirmation returned to
the Wythe County Court from the Roane County Court spells the names
Byram Breeding and Jane Breeding. I have not found a marriage record of
Byron Breeding to Nancy Breeding, however from more than one family source
I have heard the story that Byron and Nancy were cousins and that the
marriage of cousins was frowned upon in Virginia. That they were from
closely related families, there is no doubt. The first mention of
Byron's second wife, Jane, is in 1805.

There was a group of Breedings in Rhea County, formerly a part of Roane
County, Tennessee. In Toe String Valley near Rhea Springs there was a
Breeding Cemetery and a Breeding School. Buried in this cemetery is
"Byram Breeding, Feb. 23, 1832 Age 60 years" and next to this grave is
"Jane Breeding, born 1772, May 23, 1844 Age 73 years." This cemetery
was removed by Tennessee Valley Authority to the Marsh Cemetery in the
early Thirties as Loudon Dam was built. The stones are still standing
but the cemetery is not being maintained. I have not had time to
research further in Rhea and Roane Counties.

B-1 Spencer Breeding, Sr.

Spencer Breeding, Sr. lived in Shenandoah County, Virginia. Tax Lists
show him as a taxpayer from 1788 to 1793. The first mention of him in
Wythe County, Virginia was 1795. That he died before 1808 is evidenced
by the following excerpt of a deed:

"Sept. 12, 1808 Spencer Breeding and Winnie, his wife, Jacob Cup and
Sylvia his wife, Wharton Nunn and Elizabeth his wife, and Nancy Breeding
the heirs and legal representatives of Spencer Breeding deceased sold
Bryant Breeding 100 A. lying on New River."

B-2 Spencer Breeding, Jr.

The first account of Spencer Breeding, Jr was his marriage to
Winefred Hurst in Shenandoah County, Virginia, on Nov. 24, 1789,
the daughter of Absalom Hurst (taken from The Hursts of Shen-
andoah by J C Hurst). The next record is from a Wythe County,
Va. deed dated Aug 1, 1802 in which Spencer Breeding sold
Spencer Breeding, Jr 110 acres "on the north side of Little
Reed Island Creek." There are several Wythe County, Va. deeds
that show Spencer Jr added on to his land holdings along New
River and Reed Island Creek. The latest Wythe Co deed I've
found of Spencer Breeding show ing his buying from William
Breeding and wife, Charity Fugate, 130 acres on the west side
of New River. The deed is dated Sep 2, 1837. Further research
should be done in Carroll and Grayson Counties to clarify the
problem of shifting county lines. I do not know if Spencer
Breeding, Jr moved from Wythe Co or who his children were.

B-3 Elizabeth Breeding

Elizabeth Breeding married Wharton Nunn. In the List of Tennessee
Pensioners, Wharton Nunn was listed as being 85 years old in 1840. The
Nunns were a companion family to the Breedings, Hursts, and Fugates.
Some of the Nunns came to Claiborne County, Tennessee, and some went into
Kentucky.

B-4 Sylvia Breeding

Sylvia Breeding married Jacob Cupp. Again there are Cupps in Claiborne
County but I don't have further records.

B-5 Nancy Breeding

Nancy Breeding listed as an heir to Spencer Breeding, Sr. in a Wythe
County, Virginia deed dated Sept. 12, 1808. Among John Breeding's private
papers was a contract signed by Nancy Breeding and Charity Fugate wherein
John Breeding was to receive a certain portion of grain and molasses from
a tract of land. It was dated 1819. Nancy Breeding moved to Claiborne
County, Tennessee, with her son, John in the Year 1825. There is no
marriage record available proving her marriage to Byron Breeding, yet it

B-5 Nancy Breeding, Cont'd.

is traditional from several sources that they were the father
and mother of John Breeding. I believe it is true. Nancy lived
on John Breeding's estate in Tennessee. She joined the Big
Springs Primitive Baptist Church in 1830. At her death she was
buried in the old Stone family cemetery on top of a hill near
Big Springs Church. The grave is marked by rough field stones
only and the date of her death is not known. Evidently there
were no further marriages.

AB-1

John Breeding was born 1-27-1797 in either Shenandoah or Wythe
County, Va. On September 30, 1819 he purchased 50 acres of land
on the "New Cut" Road that leads from New River to Makes Creek,
from Elisha Nunn and Delily, his wife (Wythe Co., Va.). A copy
of this deed is among Joyn's private papers. In 1825 he moved
to Claiborne County, Tennessee and settled on Barren Creek near
his Uncle Bryants. He purchased land in the area between Ball
Creek and Sycamore Creek, accumulating approximately 1,200 acres.
He joined Big Speings Curch on December 1, 1833. His home was
about two miles east of Lone Mountain, Tennessee, and was a
2-story log structure. All of John's children and their marriages are known. John, and Elizabeth, his wife, were first
burried in Johnston Cemetery on Ball Creek and in the early
thirties were moved by the Tennessee Valley Authority to a
cmetery in Kettle Hollow in Union County, Tennessee. The stone,
a carved limestone from his farm, still stands and is legible

APPENDIX M

AUTHOR'S PATERNAL LINEAGE FROM BYRON BREEDING

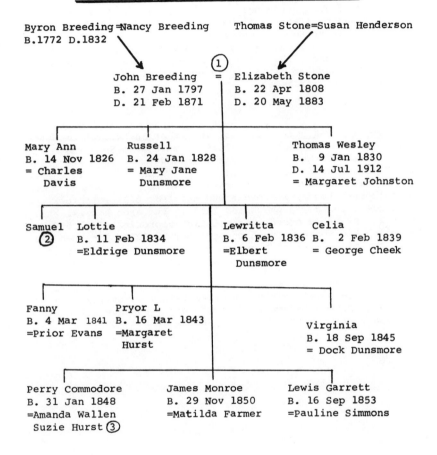

Byron Breeding = Nancy Breeding   Thomas Stone = Susan Henderson
B.1772 D.1832

(1)

John Breeding   =   Elizabeth Stone
B. 27 Jan 1797   B. 22 Apr 1808
D. 21 Feb 1871   D. 20 May 1883

Mary Ann   Russell   Thomas Wesley
B. 14 Nov 1826   B. 24 Jan 1828   B. 9 Jan 1830
= Charles   = Mary Jane   D. 14 Jul 1912
  Davis   Dunsmore   = Margaret Johnston

Samuel   Lottie   Lewritta   Celia
(2)   B. 11 Feb 1834   B. 6 Feb 1836   B. 2 Feb 1839
           =Eldrige Dunsmore   =Elbert   = George Cheek
                                Dunsmore

Fanny   Pryor L
B. 4 Mar 1841   B. 16 Mar 1843   Virginia
=Prior Evans   =Margaret   B. 18 Sep 1845
                   Hurst   = Dock Dunsmore

Perry Commodore   James Monroe   Lewis Garrett
B. 31 Jan 1848   B. 29 Nov 1850   B. 16 Sep 1853
=Amanda Wallen   =Matilda Farmer   =Pauline Simmons
 Suzie Hurst (3)

---

(1) Married January 1826

(2) Samuel and Sadie Evans Breeding were the author's
    paternal great-grand-parents. Refer to next page.

(3) Perry Commodore Breeding was married twice

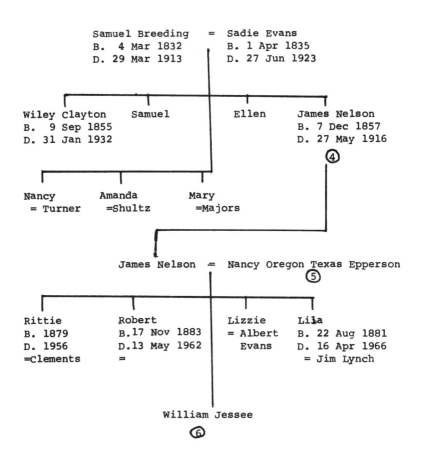

Samuel Breeding　　=　Sadie Evans
B.　4 Mar 1832　　　B. 1 Apr 1835
D. 29 Mar 1913　　　D. 27 Jun 1923

Wiley Clayton　　Samuel　　　　Ellen　　James Nelson
B.　9 Sep 1855　　　　　　　　　　　　　B. 7 Dec 1857
D. 31 Jan 1932　　　　　　　　　　　　　D. 27 May 1916
④

Nancy　　　　Amanda　　　Mary
= Turner　　=Shultz　　=Majors

James Nelson　=　Nancy Oregon Texas Epperson
⑤

Rittie　　　　Robert　　　　Lizzie　　Lila
B. 1879　　　B.17 Nov 1883　= Albert　B. 22 Aug 1881
D. 1956　　　D.13 May 1962　　Evans　D. 16 Apr 1966
=Clements　　=　　　　　　　　　　　　= Jim Lynch

William Jessee
⑥

---

④　James Nelson Breeding and Nancy Oregon Texas Epperson
　　were the author's paternal grand-parents

⑤　Please refer to page 273 for her birth date, death date
　　and parentage

⑥　William Jessee Breeding was the author's father.
　　Please refer to next page.

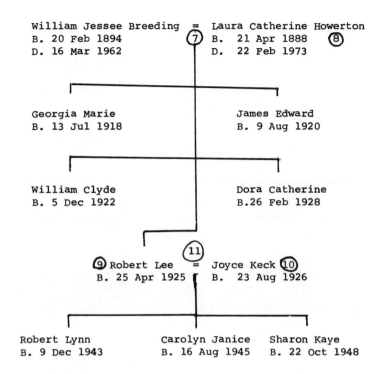

William Jessee Breeding ⑦ Laura Catherine Howerton
B. 20 Feb 1894   B. 21 Apr 1888   ⑧
D. 16 Mar 1962   D. 22 Feb 1973

Georgia Marie   James Edward
B. 13 Jul 1918   B. 9 Aug 1920

William Clyde   Dora Catherine
B. 5 Dec 1922   B.26 Feb 1928

                    ⑪
            ⑨ Robert Lee = Joyce Keck ⑩
              B. 25 Apr 1925   B. 23 Aug 1926

Robert Lynn   Carolyn Janice   Sharon Kaye
B. 9 Dec 1943   B. 16 Aug 1945   B. 22 Oct 1948

---

⑦ Married 22 Jun 1917
⑧ Please refer to page **273** for her parentage
⑨ The Author
⑩ Please refer to page 273 for her parentage
⑪ Married 22 Jan 1943

NOTES

(5) Nancy Oregon Texas Epperson was born 4 Mar 1859 died 19 Dec 1902. Her mother was Sadie (Brown) Epperson, born 19 May 1837 and died 13 Jul 1906. Her father was J. J. Epperson (no birth or death date known by the author).

(8) Marjorie Breeding, 109 E. Vance, Oak Ridge, Tn 37830 provided the following information, as well as that in Note 11 below:

Wm. Howerton, Jr
B. 1812

John Howerton   =   Mary (Polly) Stansberry
B. 1837   B. 28 Aug 1840
D. 1907   D. 21 Jan 1921

Wm. Brownlow Howerton = (11) Lou Vesta Myers
B. 19 Oct 1860   B. 6 Jul 1863
D. 4 Mar 1935   D. 22 Feb 1934

John   Greene   Laura   Roxie Tennessee Hedi

(10) Jonathan Esau Keck   =   Rebecca Lynch
B. 31 May 1878   B. 31 May 1880
D. 4 Nov 1967   D. 7 Oct 1944

Isaac Newton Keck   = (12) Christie Elgie Davis
B. 7 Dec 1902   B. 21 Apr 1903
D. 10 Jun 1971   D. 11 Feb 1976

Weir Bruce   Joyce   Ross G.   Stanley E.

(11) Her parents were John Myers, born 1824 in Hancock County, Tennessee and Arminda Carpenter, born 1826 presumably in Hancock County

(12) Her parents were Bert Davis, born 1 Mar 1877 and died 9 Dec 1960, and Dora Greer, born 28 Oct 1870 and died 2 Sep 1924.

APPENDIX   K

A pictoral representation of a Cherokee village of the early eighteenth century (distributed by Fidelity Federal Savings and Loan Association in 1978). Also refer to next page.

CHOTA, CAPITAL OF THE CHEROKEE NATION

Another artist's conception of a Cherokee village of the time accompanied Dr. Duane H. King's article, "A Wall to the Skies," printed in a brochure entitled "Unto These Hills," Cherokee Historical Association, Cherokee, North Carolina, 1977.

ABOUT THE AUTHOR

This book is about the heritage of the southern high-lander, who is known to most of the nation as a hillbilly. I know the author to be one of the, just as I am.

I first knew Robert Breeding in 1941 when I was principal of Claiborne County High School in Tazewell, Tennessee and he was fifteen and a junior. As a senior, I remember, he stood out from among his classmates—not because he was handsome or well-dressed but because he was a good student and a hard worker who exhibited an extraordinary zeal to learn. He became Vice-President of the senior class, President of the Beta Club, and volunteered for every extra academic activity offered. When his fellow students finished their school day and went home, however, Robert turned to his tasks of sweeping the floors, cleaning the coal stoves, and preparing to build fires next morning. That was the way he earned the money necessary for his books, clothing, and other school expenses.

Although I was not intimately acquainted with Robert's family, I knew the general area where he was born and reared to be one of the most geographically remote in the county. In addition, it was said that the area had more than its share of people who were deliberately clannish, inflexible in their lifestyle, and suspicious of outsiders. Also, I was told that the population was in the lower quartile for its youth's completion of elementary grades of schooling.

Our paths were separated by World War II, but in 1946, when I was an administrator at The University of Tennessee and Robert a student there, we became re-acquainted. I saw him commissioned in the Air Force, graduate from the university, and begin to teach in a local high school. Shortly thereafter I learned that he had returned to military life. We continued to keep in touch, however, and he usually visited me when he was *home*. As I grew in my work at The University of Tennessee I saw Robert travel widely in the United States, Europe, and the Far East; study in four or five major universities; teach either full-time or in the Evening College of eight or ten colleges or universities; promoted regularly and retired as a Lieutenant Colonel; and return *home* to an aministrative job with the University of Tennessee. Through all those years I had the feeling that he considered himself an authentic hillbilly or southern highlander, and that he was proud of it.

It is unquestionably his love and respect for his people and mine that has led him to investigate their general origin and ancestry, and he has done so in the style of the professional researcher that he is. He is quite vociferous and adamant that he wrote this book to show the world that his people (and mine) are happy and proud in a world of their own making, and that they are hillbillies and mountain-people, so-to-speak, mainly because they want to be. And for the same reasons many of their offspring will remain in their beloved southern highland hideaway— simply because that is what they want to do.

Dr. Breeding is a product of the mountains, has spent many years away from *home,* and is now back among his people. Whereas, I am also a product of the southern highlands but have spent my life on the fringes of the area trying to "help our own." Both of us believe, however, that we know the truth of the saying that "to know our people is to know how to enjoy life." Although I am not so inclined, Dr. Breeding tells me that he finds no greater joy and pleasure than to visit with his hillbilly friends from the old days, play checkers around the coal stove in the country store, go fishing, attend a hoedown, or just sit and talk while whittling on a piece of red cedar.

J. E. Arnold

JAMES E. ARNOLD, Ed.D.
Dean Emeritus
The University of Tennessee

Dr. James E. Arnold was retired from The University of Tennessee in 1972 as Dean of Continuing Education for The University of Tennessee State-wide system, and he presently spends much of his time attending his registered Angus and Hereford cattle on his Holston River farm near Knoxville. He is a two-term Tennessee State Senator and a nationally known educator, having been presented the Nolte Award for excellence in Continuing Education. The 38th edition of *WHO'S WHO* notes, among other things, that he was born in Sneedville, Tennessee (Hancock County), is married to Grace Harrison, and has two children. He earned a B.A. at Carson-Newman College and an M.A. and Edd. at The University of Tennessee. He has served as the principal of three Tennessee high schools and in the administration of The University of Tennessee for twenty-seven years. He is a former member and chairman of a long and impressive list of organizations, and even in semiretirement he served as Executive Director of the Clinch-Powell Educational Cooperative, with offices at Lincoln Memorial University.